Hotel Chronicles

Melissa Elizabeth

Please direct all copyright inquiries to:
B.O.Y. Enterprises, Inc.
c/o Author Copyrights
P.O. Box 1012
Lowell, NC 28098

Cover and Interior Design: B.O.Y. Enterprises, Inc.

Paperback ISBN: 978-1-955605-05-2

Printed in the United States.

Dedication

This book is affectionately dedicated to my loving mother, Priscilla Prayer. Thank you for being an example of love, strength, and loyalty.

Thank you, Mommy.

Table of Contents

Introduction

As I looked around, I never would have thought I would still be in this place; a place that has gone through numerous renovations to keep up with the swanky vibe these new hotels have. The lobby alone has changed from a seventies flare with stone fireplaces and swivel chairs to funky chaise lounges and fire pits. It seems as if I, along with the regulars who stay with us, continuously try to renovate ourselves in order to keep up. Since I was little, I have always tried to blend into my surroundings, to attract as little attention as possible. Like a chameleon, changing myself has become second nature. You see, what started out as a side gig to help me make some money until my career took off, has turned into 15 years of complacent monotony. Albeit entertaining monotony, it is monotony, nonetheless.

I grew up in Montclair, NJ with parents who worked hard and became rather successful. They tried to instill this same work ethic within their two children and believed that opting out of college was not an option. I never had the ambition or drive like my older brother and went through life doing just enough to get by. My parents would always say to me, "Morgan, you could be doing so much more."

I treated the idea of doing more like the plague. I hated high school and certainly wasn't feeling college. So, when my parents sat me down and forced me to decide on a major, I picked communications. I figured, hell I like to talk, so why not make some money doing it. They then proceeded to research the top colleges that had excellent communications programs. For them, money was no object when it came to college.

See, in many middle-class black families, college is such a priority that parents begin saving for it when their child is very young (sometimes while they are still in the womb). I believe my parents knew early off that I was not scholarship material so I think they put as much extra in the kitty as they could. I ended up graduating from the University of Maryland skating by with just enough so my parents could save face with their friends. I certainly didn't want the, "you know how hard mom and dad worked to get you to college speech," from my older brother. So, I vowed not to flunk out but mustered up enough motivation to try only as hard as necessary.

After college, I took a year to travel and "find myself". The only thing I found was that I was broke and had no life ambitions. When I got home, my Dad seized what he perceived as an opportunity to help me earn some money so that I could get back on my feet before jumping into my career in communications. He had a friend who was a manager at a hotel. It was a guaranteed job that I saw as a way to earn some money to move to California and enjoy the outdoors. Mom had hoped I would attract the attention a young upwardly mobile man and get married. But at twenty-one, I had neither the desire, swag, nor even the scent to attract a bee let alone a man.

So here I am today a man-less, middle-aged woman who is in such a lifelong rut that I feel like a hamster just going around and around in their running wheel; only I'm not running I'm walking because ya girl doesn't do sweat. At this stage of life though, I desperately want to stop the wheel, but I just don't know how to take that one leap to get off. I'd love to be able to finally say I am going to make a life change and there is no turning back. I yearn to throw caution to the wind and enter a new dimension of my life... a dimension where I live life for me and not for my bills, my parents, or my job.

I wonder if that dimension even exists. Is there a place where I have self-worth and feel excited to wake up each morning and start my next daily adventure? Could life ever be about happiness and not contentment? Can true joy replace complacency? Could I ever exist in a space and time where I meet the man of my dreams and we travel and just enjoy life together?

"Ahh excuse me. Ma'am. Hello!"

Suddenly I was jolted back to reality.

"Yes?"

"I have a reservation."

Chapter One:

Let Me Introduce Myself

I came out of my trance to see in front of me a tall muscular man who looked like he just stepped off the cover of Men's Fitness. I mean if Calvin Klein needed another underwear model, he would be it. I was stunned at the hunk of manly awesomeness that was standing in front of me. Every muscle, peck, and curve were perfectly protruding in all the right places. His arms were succulently saying I will wrap you in heaven, his chiseled face and luscious lips screamed sex appeal, and his jeans were carefully hugging his man muscle giving you a hint of how endowed he really was. I was speechless but trying not to let my mouth hang open.

"Uh ma'am, are you okay?"

"Uh yes," I managed to squeak out. "Your name please."

"Giorgio Donato," he purred with a sexy smile.

Even his name sounded dreamy! Who is this gorgeous creature in front of me and does he even see me? I mean really see me. Or does he see just an ordinary desk clerk who has the capacity to give him the best room we have and all the hospitable accommodations that come with it? Is he thinking about what my lips can do to him like I'm thinking about what I want his to do to me?

I proceeded to check him in thinking of what first floor room would be the best place to put him in so he would have to walk past the front desk to get to everything; all the while trying not to show my shaky hands. What a treat it would be to watch him pass the front desk getting ice, going to the pool, or exercise room. To watch him as he works in the business center or sits at the bar sipping a drink would be the highlight of my week. This just might turn out to be a good night.

All of a sudden, the front door slid open and a woman with a crying baby in one arm and tugging a little boy with her other arm entered. She clearly looked agitated and ready to bite someone's head off. She stomped over to the man and began yelling at him. "What the hell is taking you so long? You know Manny is hungry and I have to feed him!"

Who did she think she was talking to my Giorgio like that? How dare she! The hunk of awesomeness rolled his eyes and gave me a smirk like can you please hurry up lady. I immediately went back to the previous computer screen changing his room from the eye candy suite to the "we have a screaming kid" suite.

Every hotel has a section of rooms which they try to reserve for the off-the-chain kids. We know those reservations will result in carpet stains, broken room items, and several front desk phone calls from complaining guests. This is the section of the hotel that is as far away from the mainstream of things and where the minimal number of repairs are done. The maintenance staff does just enough to make things look aesthetically pleasing because we know they are just going to get broken or messed up again. Maintenance and Housekeeping know they will have to spend a little more time in those rooms because folks let their bratty kids run amuck in them. They have to look more carefully for juice-stained towels and linens, crayons shoved in the seats and couches, and little toys hidden behind beds and in drawers.

"Ms. Evilena" marched over to the lounge and plopped down on one of the plush couches and proceeded to whip out her breast which the baby quickly devoured. The little boy saw the opportunity to escape and ran over to the fountain. He took both his hands and began to splash water all over the place. The cute Asian couple, waiting for the shuttle to take them downtown, looked horrified and quickly made a beeline for the door. They decided it was probably safer to wait outside because the wife was not trying to get wet and hubby didn't need a peep show.

"Thank you, Mr. Donato. Your room number is 323 and the elevator is to your right. Do you need anyone to assist you with your bags?"

"That won't be necessary," he said, just wanting to get out of there. He screamed for his wife and son to come on and they headed towards the elevator.

Melissa Elizabeth

"Wow!" I said to Sebastian, the other assistant on duty.

"Oh yeah honey, wow is right! I'll be his wifey any day! And the only screams he'll hear when he's with me will be screams of pleasure!" Sebastian blurted out as he fanned himself. He acted like he was going to faint as he headed to the back office. Sebastian was a diva and had all the drama to go with the title.

Slightly disappointed, I thought, well a girl can dream, right? As I was sulking behind the counter, a man assisting an elderly woman walked in. He helped her to the closest chair and proceeded to the counter.

"Good evening sir. How can I help you?"

"I need a room for my mom, please," he said as he glanced over at the chair to ensure she was okay.

"How long will she be staying?"

"I am not sure, probably a week."

"Okay, no problem. Her name please."

He went on to tell me that his father just died and his mother, Margaret Stein, refused to stay in the house they built 55 years ago. He hoped this was just a phase. That maybe she would miss her husband so much she would want to go back there just to be close to him and the memories they shared there.

"I'm so sorry to hear about the passing of your father. Is there anything we can do to make your mother's stay more comfortable?"

"Uh yes, she will need a smoking room please."

"I apologize, but we are a non-smoking facility. We have several outdoor spaces where smoking is permitted, but your mother will not be able to smoke in her room."

He shrugged his shoulders. "Oh well. She'll have to adjust. Give her a first-floor room please. She has trouble walking sometimes."

After checking her in and giving him the room key, he helped his mother out the chair, placed his mouth an inch away from her ear and screamed, "You're all set Mom. Let me take you to your room!"

She yelled back, "Tommy get my things!"

This petite elderly woman dressed in a St. John suit and Tods shoes proceeded to whip out a cigarette and lighter from her purse and begun smoking. She couldn't get the cancer stick to her mouth fast enough. I went from around the counter and escorted her to the veranda letting her know that smoking was not allowed in the building, but she could go out there anytime to smoke. I sat her down on the lounge chair and let her know I would get her when her son returned. She smiled at me and for the first time I looked into her eyes. In only a split second I could see that there was more behind this woman than what could be seen on the exterior. Her eyes displayed a softness and an almost pleading look that I couldn't describe. I immediately sensed a connection with her. Those eyes looked all too familiar. I just couldn't put my finger on it. What do they mean? What are they really saying? I knew right then I would find out as much as I could about her story.

The son, now back in the lobby wearing an agitated expression, grabbed the dolly located by the front door and went outside. After about 15 minutes I began to wonder if he was even coming back. About 20 minutes later, he came in with a trunk, 5 suitcases, a large plant, and a golden vase like structure that was safely placed between two vertical suitcases. I was confused. Who needs that much stuff for one week?

Upon seeing the vase, the lady stumbled in from the patio screaming, "Give me Harry!" The man looked like he was about to cuss her out but carefully removed the vase and placed it in her hands. She took what I realized was urn and cradled it in her arm like someone carrying a baby.

Sebastian gave me the raised eyebrow glance and that "you gotta be kidding me" look. I covered my mouth to keep from laughing. Mrs. Stein carefully followed behind her son as he made his way toward her room.

"I know that dead man's ashes ain't up in that vase," Sebastian said under his breath as soon as they were out of earshot.

I just giggled and thought to myself, I better let housekeeping know.

A few minutes later a young woman walked in and proceeded to walk around the lobby as if she was looking for someone. She didn't look a day over 21 but was dressed in a business suit that was so tight it looked like every button on her jacket could pop off at any minute relieving her suffocating breasts. Her skirt was so tight and short it looked like the seams were hanging together for dear life. After circling the lobby several times, all the while texting vigorously on her phone, I asked if I could help her.

"Yes, I am meeting a Mr. Giorgio Donato here. Can you tell me if he has checked in yet?"

"Ma'am I am sorry, but we are not permitted to give out any guest information."

"Well, I see his car outside, so I know he is here. Can you give me his room number?"

"Once again, we are not permitted to give out any guest information."

The young woman rolled her eyes and immediately commanded her phone to call Giorgio's cell. I then heard her speak into her earpiece asking the caller on the other line where they were. It appeared that she had gotten the person's machine for she proceeded to say that she was at the hotel waiting in the lobby. She ended with the demand for a call back as soon as possible for she couldn't wait to see him. The sultry tone in her voice clearly let me know this was not a business meeting.

I immediately became intrigued and realized that this just might be an even more interesting night than I originally imagined. Watch eye candy strut by is fun, but juicy drama trumps lust any day of the week.

Melissa Elizabeth

The young woman sashayed over to a nearby couch (the same one that was the breastfeeding zone two hours ago) and carefully maneuvered her slender body down in it (you could tell that her skirt issue was making it difficult to sit comfortably).

Suddenly, she jumped up and screamed, "Honey, there you are!"

I looked up to see Mr. Donato rounding the corner as the ping of the elevator doors could be heard behind him. The look of shock and displeasure began to cover his face. The young lady ran over and tried to give him a kiss. He stretched his arms to block the impact and ushered her over to the corner carefully looking over his shoulder.

"Hey baby, what are you doing here? You didn't get my message?" he whispered.

"No, what message?"

"I left you a message saying something came up and we would have to reschedule."

She clearly looked disappointed.

"Aww baby we haven't had our time together in over a month and I miss you." She was slowly gliding her hands up and down his ripped abs and chest. I felt a slight pang of jealousy as her hand movements reminded me just how long it had been since I felt a man's hard chest beneath my hands.

Trying to control her hands he pleaded, "Look baby, now is not a good time. You have to leave."

"If you cancelled our date, then what are you doing here?" she inquired as she abruptly removed her hands and transitioned into what looked like a defensive stance.

Sebastian walked over to the edge of the front desk to get a closer view. Neither one of us bothered trying to pretend like we weren't watching and listening to every word they spoke. We were both wondering how this dude was going to handle this one.

Not wanting to get her upset he stated that he would try and move some of his obligations around so they can have an enjoyable evening.

"Do you see how he side stepped her question?" Sebastian whispered to me.

"You know I did," I whispered back.

Giorgio walked her over to the front desk and asked Sebastian for a room. Sebastian paused as if to say, you really want to do this, but figured, hey it's your life. Sebastian proceeded to get Mr. Donato a second room for him and his mistress. Mr. Donato asks if there is a room available on the north side of the hotel making the excuse that it gets less sun.

Sebastian shot me a Less-sun-my-ass look, and I had to suppress a laugh.

"Yeah, I hear the heat on the south side ain't nothing to play with and it's probably about to get a whole lot hotter," Sebastian chimed, giving him the side eye.

Mr. Donato chuckled uncomfortably and handed him his credit card. Once his got his second set of keys, he handed them to the young woman.

"Look Jess, why don't you go to the room and get comfortable. I need to take care of some things in the business center and I will be there shortly."

"Sure baby." She kissed him on the cheek and headed to the same elevator Mr. Donato just came out of.

Sebastian stopped her. "Uh ma'am, the elevator over on the other side is closer to your room." He gave Mr. Donato a "you owe me" smirk and sashayed back to the counter in true diva fashion.

Mr. Donato rubbed his forehead and let out a sigh. "There was a water main break in front of our house," he began. "The city turned off the water for the whole block, but not before it backed up into my front yard. Thankfully it didn't make it into the house, but with two kids, there was no way we could stay at home with no water. I figured since I already had the reservation, I could just call Jess off and spend the night here with my family. Tomorrow the water will be back on and we can go home. I just have to survive tonight."

I realized he wasn't really talking to me. He was trying to calm his own nerves and since I wasn't in the business of soothing cheaters, I kept my mouth shut

"It's only for one night. It's only for one night," he chanted to himself.

I wanted to say, "that's what you get you cheating bastard," but I restrained myself again, keeping my face from showing the disappointment and disgust I was feeling.

Sebastian mumbled, "Uh you certainly have your hands full."

Mr. Donato clearly looking distraught glanced back and forth not sure which room to go to first. He decided he should check on his wife and kids, so he made a beeline to the elevator he had just came out of.

Sebastian sashayed to the back-office yelling, "Let me make some popcorn! We are in for a show tonight!"

The phone rang and I took several deep breaths to keep myself from laughing before I answered it. As I am on the phone, I see Mrs. Stein bundled up in her fur coat puffing away on the outside patio. It's times like this that I am thankful that I never had any desire to smoke anything. I had a great fear of becoming addicted to anything. I hate not being in control. Besides, I was afraid of ending up like Halle Berry on Jungle Fever. The image of such a beautiful woman turning into a skinny crack head junkie proved to be the best "Just Say No" ad for many young black women. We all strived to be the beautiful and successful Angela who nailed Marcus Graham, played by Eddie Murphy, in Boomerang; not the drug addict Vivian prostituting her body so her and Gator Purify, played by Samuel L. Jackson, can get high.

It was so cold outside poor Mrs. Stein's hands were shaking, or maybe that was the onset of Parkinson's. Either way, I felt sorry for her. I hung up the phone and told Sebastian I would be right back. I got my coat and joined Mrs. Stein.

"Can I let you in on a little secret?" I said.

"Sure," Mrs. Stein replied as the cigarette hung from her lips.

"I know the secret on how to smoke in your room without setting off the smoke detectors."

I ain't never seen an old woman move so fast. Mrs. Stein nearly fell in the fire pit trying to get closer to me.

"But you have to promise me you will not tell a soul," I pleaded.

"Girl, I won't even tell Harry!"

I proceeded to let her know that if she stood by the heater with the air on full blast and the window fully open, the smoke would never stay in the room but immediately go out the window. As long as she directed all the smoke towards the window it would never be detected. I did state the disclaimer that if for some reason the detector did go off and the sprinkler system ruined all her things, I or the hotel would not be held responsible. I told her that this conversation never existed, and she would be on her own.

As she gave me this big bear hug of gratitude, I could smell the smoke stench all in her ruby red hair and flowy mink coat. What a travesty! Such a beautiful specimen of clothing ruined by years of addiction. Oh yeah, not to mention what it was doing to her body. I suddenly felt bad that I cared more about the effects the cigarettes were having on the mink then what it was doing to her health. That feeling of guilt lasted about two seconds.

Mrs. Stein discarded her barely used cigarette. She couldn't wait to get out the cold and try out her newly discovered secret. I smiled and quickly proceeded back to the front desk before Sebastian could send out the search squad. If he felt I was taking too long on one of my unscheduled breaks he would immediately do an "APB" on the walkie and have the whole staff looking for me. Or he would make up a wild story of where I was and what I was doing and announce it over the walkie for all to speculate as to whether he was really telling the truth. Sometimes it would take weeks of denial before I could get them to really understand that what he said was just a figment of his active and crazy imagination.

"Girl, where you been? Do you know that dog had the nerve to call down here and ask me to ring his mistress's room and tell her to order them a late dinner from room service! I wanted to tell him to do his own dirty work, but he offered me twenty dollars."

"Sebastian, I know you didn't call that girl's room!"

"Honey, I told him make it thirty and I will deliver the dinner myself."

Just then the elevator doors opened and out stomped Mrs. Donato with baby and little boy in tow. She was yelling at her husband that she would not stay in that room another minute.

"But Baby, I just ordered some pizzas and thought we would eat in the room. I figured you would be too tired to eat downstairs." Mr. Donato was running to catch up with her.

"I am not eating pizza when the hotel has a wonderful restaurant," She said as she headed for the restaurant.

Mr. Donato looked around, shrugged his shoulders, and gave us a fifty-dollar bill. "Here, dinner is on me." He made a quick call upstairs to inform his lover that he was currently working in the business center and would be up in about an hour. He then sprinted to meet his wife.

I think to myself-really Giorgio, is this all worth it. Meanwhile Sebastian was grinning from ear to ear, hoping the man didn't order anchovies on the pizza.

About thirty minutes later I saw Mistress Jess walking through the lobby. I hit Sebastian who immediately looked up ready to cuss me out. I pointed before he could utter a word.

"Ahhhh sukie sukie now! Let the fun begin!" he chuckled as he hurried to grab his popcorn.

I tried to divert her by saying, "Excuse me Miss, can I help you?"

She ignored me, looked into the business center, and then finally acknowledged me with a puzzled stare.

"Ummm, I was looking for someone, but I guess he stepped out. Can you show me how to get to the bar? I think I need a drink."

I began to stutter not knowing how to handle this situation. If I told her she would surely run into her cheating man and his wife.

Sebastian rushed back to my side with is popcorn in hand. "It is right over there," he said as he pointed towards the restaurant.

I gave him a look like he was crazy. "Maybe you should try the new Sports Bar down the street. Drinks are ½ off tonight, you can get free appetizers during happy hour, and the bar tenders are heavy handed on the liquor."

She paid me no attention. "Thanks Sebastian," she said as she headed to the bar which is conveniently located within the restaurant.

Sebastian grabbed my arm and said, "Come on, I ain't missing this one!"

We didn't even make it inside the restaurant before we heard the commotion. Sebastian sped up, and I quickly matched his stride. Upon arriving we saw "Jess the Mess" standing over "Giorgio the Gigolo" screaming, "What the hell do you think you are doing?"

Mr. Donato nearly choked. He stood up and tried to move away.

His wife stood up and yelled at Jess, "Who do you think you are talking to my husband like that?"

"Your husband? Oh really!" Jess then looked at Mr. Donato, gave him a smirk, and walked over to Mrs. Donato. "Allow me to introduce myself. I am the woman your husband has been having sex with for the last few months. In fact," she said as she leaned in closer to Mrs. Donato, "if you kissed him when he came home late last Thursday night, you probably smelled me on his breath."

Without a word, the motherly Mrs. Donato disappeared, and a bar room brawler took over her body. In a split-second Jess ricocheted off the neighboring table and landed face down on the ground, knocked out cold. Everyone was stunned as Mr. Donato ran over to check on the other woman. Mrs. Donato, still remaining silent, picked up the baby, grabbed the little boy's hand, and walked out. She only paused for a split second to kick Mr. Donato in the groin with her stilettoes. All the men present immediately groaned and protectively grabbed down there as if they might be next.

Sebastian and I ran back to the unattended front desk and began to replay the scene. I was Mrs. Donato punching Sebastian as he dramatically fell back onto the desk and

25

then dropped to the floor. We did this several times, sometimes even in slow motion. I was laughing so hard I didn't even notice Mrs. Donato as she dumped a pile of clothes and other things onto the floor of the front lobby. When I finally composed myself and wiped away the tears of laughter, I saw Jess leaving the restaurant crying and screaming. She yelled, "I never want to see you again," before she bolted onto the elevator.

Mr. Donato slowly walked out, looked at his things sprawled across the lobby floor, and meandered over to the front desk. He plopped his credit card onto the counter and said, "I need a room please."

Chapter Two:

The Circle of Life

I stood in Room 716 watching a guest go through every inch of the room pointing out the lack of cleanliness that she stated to be evident within her room. I mean really. Who goes through a hotel room, with a white glove on, rubbing every nook and cranny looking for dirt to appear on their finger? She was lucky I cared about my reputation as a professional because she nearly earned herself a beat down when she showed me the dust she found from rubbing her middle finger on the back of the headboard. I knew she was saying "F-you" but I gave her a one-time only pass. I patiently waited for her to finish, acting as if I was really interested.

Sebastian and I say folks like this have OCD- either obsessive compulsive disorder or Out for Complimentary Dividends (which basically means if you make such a ruckus you get it free). Once the tour over, I apologized to the woman, explained that the hotel was booked and suggested that she go downstairs and have a complimentary meal in our restaurant while I get someone to up here to address her concerns.

I would have given her just about anything to get her out of my face. I could hear Ana, our head housekeeper, cussing me out in Spanish as I asked her to send someone to Room 716 stat. I never had a desire to learn Spanish in high school, but I sure wished I knew it when Ana went on her rants. Leaving the room, I wondered if this was indication of how my full shift was going to go. I hoped it wasn't. There was nothing worse than a hotel full of nitpicky, trouble-making guests.

As I walked to the elevator, I saw a woman struggling to get on it with a huge double side-by-side stroller. There were two crying kids strapped in it and two other little ones pushing all the number buttons on the elevator. I helped her gently lift the stroller whose front two wheels seem to have gotten stuck thus preventing it from moving forward. As the stroller took up most of the elevator space, I thought about just waiting for the next one but realized I better get on in case this sucker gets stuck from all 13 buttons being pushed. I made sure I had my walkie and reached for my pocket to ensure I had my cell phone. If I had to be stuck on the elevator, I wanted to make sure I was prepared to arrange a speedy rescue.

So, I squeezed myself in and waited for us to stop at every floor from 6 on down praying that no one else tried to squeeze in. I proceeded to watch as this poor woman began to loudly "shh" them in order to calm them down while trying to grab the hands of the other two who were now jumping up and down saying "weeee." It took all of my energy to remain quiet. All I could think was where was their damn binkie and their daddy's belt. Both things a black momma always had extras of and kept on standby. Clearly, she missed the memo.

We finally got down to the lobby. I was so anxious to get off the elevator that I almost forgot to help the lady with her stroller. The two toddlers bolted out the door and ran towards the complimentary cookies grabbing four at a time. Sebastian and I looked at each other thinking we better ration out these cookies while these heathens are around. They then bolted for the front door while their mom was yelling at them from behind. Her cries to slow down and wait for her fell on deaf ears.

"That's why I ain't having no kids," said Sebastian shaking his head in dismay.

I saw Ethel, our front desk clerk, look over at me to see what I would say. Sweet Ethel, who we often referred to as church lady, was always trying to get me to come to her church and the events the single ministry would put on monthly. She assured me that I would meet my future husband there and be able to settle down and have kids. I would tease her and tell her I was never getting married and would be an old spinster with 10 cats.

I knew I was on display, but I refused to take the bait. I simply responded with an "oh yeah" and went into my office to try and call Ana.

It was times like these that caused me to wonder if I was mom material. I wondered if I would even find someone in time to be able to have kids. The timeline has gone through my head so many times:

I'd meet someone then spend 2-3 years dating, then another 2 years being engaged. Of course, we'd want to enjoy each other and work out the kinks of a new marriage for the first 2-3 years before we even considered having children. Then, add on another year or so to conceive and carry the child, and damn... I'd be looking at a minimum of 9 years! I'd be well within my forties and frankly who wants to be nursing babies at 46 years old. A minimum of 9 years makes me think of a prison sentence. Why is it that in our society marriage must always lead into having children? Like your marriage ain't legit if you don't have children. Church lady Ethel states, "Malachi 2:15 tells us that He seeks godly offspring." Well heck, even if I do have offspring, I don't know how godly their gonna be!

Part of me wants the all-American black dream – to be featured in Essence magazine as the power couple who can have it all: success, money, and family. But the other part of me doesn't want to get caught up in dreaming about a fantasy that may never come to fruition which then leads to disappointment and heartbreak. So, I just accept in my mind that I don't want it and that maternal feeling that sometimes rises up in my heart gets forced deep down into the pit of my soul never to be stirred up again.

You know the feeling you get when you see a stylish black woman walking with her adorable little girl dressed like her "mini me?" You know the feeling you get when you hear an excited little voice shout, "Mommy?" You know that feeling when you see the cute image of two chubby hands grabbing the cheeks of their momma and pulling her in for a kiss? You know the feeling you get when your friend on Facebook is always sharing those "melt your heart" photos of these beautiful babies that look like porcelain dolls? That feeling. The older I got the easier it became to suppress them because I knew the outcome would be because of my biological clock and not as a result of my inability to open up and let anyone in. It would be because of the nature of the way God made us and not because of the fact that I'm unlovable or incapable of love.

"Señora Morgan…Señora Morgan…Are you there?"

The voice of Ana over the walkie pulled me out of my trance.

"Si," I say over the walkie?

"What is the room number again?"

I told her the number and decided to go out and check on the front desk. As soon as I walked out of my office, Ethel grabbed me.

"Oh, Ms. Morgan I was just about to come get you. Sebastian is on his break and honey my water pills are working! Can you stay here while I run to the bathroom?"

"Sure Ethel. I got you." This came as a much-needed distraction from the thoughts going on in my head.

She did a few more shakes that let me know she better hurry or I'll be calling housekeeping for a mop, then rushed to the nearest bathroom. As I watched her hustle away, I noticed an older gentleman holding the front door for a young pregnant woman who looked like she was about to pop any minute. I thought to myself I can't believe this dirty old man still has it in him to be poppin' out babies let alone with someone who looks like she can be his granddaughter. I tried to keep my face from betraying me and telling him exactly what I was thinking.

The woman waddled over to the counter with her rolling suitcase in tow. As I proceeded to look up her reservation, I asked her how far along is she. She told me that she was one week overdue and that this was her first child. She told me that she had been trying to get her boyfriend to finish the nursery for weeks and he finally decided to finish it this morning. I thought to myself, you mean "Pops" didn't even have the decency to marry you? I quickly shoved the thought out of my mind. The last thing I needed was a complaint for judging the couple.

He decided he was going to install a high-tech wireless monitoring system. "Don't you know this idiot blew a fuse and now we have no electricity!"

Wow, that's how she talked about him when he was standing right there. She went on to say she could not stay in that scorching hot apartment, so her mom got her this room for the night. You mean, this dude couldn't even pay for the room? No longer able to hide my emotions, I looked at him with disgust and wondered what she was in him if he wasn't her sugar daddy.

I asked her for a credit card and she hesitantly reached in her purse for her wallet. She asked me if her card would be charged immediately or once she checked out. That statement immediately puts any front desk attendant on guard. We quickly think these people might be running a scam. I informed her that we must have a card on file and that she won't be charged until the following morning for her room and any other incidentals. She smiled with a sigh of relief and told me that her mom was coming later, and she would replace her card information with her mom's. With some apprehension I said okay but told her to make sure it was done before 5 am tomorrow morning.

"Sure," she said.

I gave her two room keys and she proceeded to gather her things.

As I proceeded to turn and walk away the silent boyfriend says, "Excuse me Miss, but I also have a reservation."

"Oh, I am so sorry I thought you two were together."

I seem to have this terrible habit of assuming things and creating life stories for people based on what I initially see. Here I had practically crucified this man thinking he was the trifling boyfriend who slept with his granddaughter's best friend. I immediately felt guilty and hoped I could quickly change my countenance towards him.

Hotel Chronicles

This bad habit started in college when my friends and I would go to the mall. We had no money so we would sit in the mall and see who could create the best story about someone walking by. We would spend hours just watching people and trying to recreate their life story. My friend Chris was so good at it you sometimes thought he knew them personally.

This gentleman was very quiet and didn't bite when I asked him probing questions like, "Are you visiting from out of town?" I just assumed he had an attitude with me because I tried to pass him off as a perverted old man who liked young girls. But then something strange happened. When I handed him his room key our eyes locked. For the first time I really saw who this guy was. His eyes showed a deep sadness. It was almost as if they were crying for help... like he was looking at me as if to say "Save Me."

A chill ran up my spine and I immediately looked towards the elevator giving him our welcome spiel including Happy Hour specials and pool times. He didn't seem the least bit interested. He did say it was going to be an early night for him and he did not want to be disturbed. As he walked away, I thought it rather strange that he only had a shopping bag from what looked like an automotive store.

My mind fantasied about him traveling home from a business trip and his car broke down. He got it towed to the nearest mechanic and they couldn't fix it until tomorrow, so he had to get a room for the night. The sadness I saw was probably the disappointment that he had

34

to wait one more day to see his wife of 43 years. He kept promising his wife this would be the year he retired. I imagined her being a sweet old lady who loved baking and watching game shows. How sad. I watched him get on the elevator and our eyes locked one more time as he waited for the door to close. I yelled, "Have a great night." He gave me a little smirk as he held tight to his shopping bag.

Sebastian walked up and said, "Umm, the way he holding that bag it must be his good night juice. Somebody don't need to come downstairs for Happy Hour when he's gonna have his own right in Room…" He looked at me and I finished his sentence.

"304!" We high fived each other. "Sebastian you're a mess."

"But you love all this mess."

"You know it."

A few hours quietly passed, and I was actually able to get some work done in my office with little interruption. That's rare but I am grateful considering I was backlogged with paperwork. The phone rung and based on its ring tone I knew it was an in-house call. It rung a few more times and I was about to fuss at the guys at the front desk to answer it, but I just picked it up. The front desk staff hated to pick up in-house calls because it usually required them to do something more than transfer a call or set up a reservation. You always took your chances when you answered a call from a guest's room because you never knew what you would get.

When I picked up all I could hear was panting. I said, "Hello, how can I help you?" about three times just to hear the panting get louder. Working in a hotel for as long as I had nothing surprised me, but I was not about to listen to a couple get their freak on. They'd have to live out their exhibitionist fantasies another way. I was just about to hang up when I heard a woman gasp, "Yes this is room 214 and I need you to call an ambulance. I think I am having my baby."

This was the woman I checked in earlier who I knew was going to pop any minute. I let her know we would call for help and someone was on their way up to her room. I ran out my office asking Sebastian to call 911 and for Ethel to send housekeeping up to 214 with lots of sheets and towels. I didn't know what to expect so my tv show knowledge kicked in.

When we arrived on the second floor all you could hear was screaming. Other guests were gathered outside the hallway with looks of fear, distain, or the "y'all better shut this damn noise up" faces. I informed them that everything was okay and that a guest was experiencing contractions. Sebastian had called 911 and was on his cell phone with them. We entered the room ready, expecting the worse, but praying for the best. The woman was sprawled out on the bed clutching the pillows and screaming in agonizing pain. I tried calming her down by letting her know the ambulance was on the way but all she could do was cuss expletives while demanding we get this baby out of her now.

Melissa Elizabeth

I thought about my days of watching Grey's Anatomy and told her to breathe. Sebastian and I propped her up with pillows and I held her hand. The 911 operator told us to start counting the minutes between contractions. The time seemed like an eternity as the minutes between each contraction quickly decreased. I kept praying, God please don't let me have to deliver a baby tonight. Within minutes the paramedics were barging in the room asking everyone to give them room. You didn't have to tell us twice. Sebastian and I immediately proceeded to get up and leave when the woman grabbed my hand and said, "Can you stay with me please?"

Ughhh, why me? Sebastian is more compassionate and soothing. Why not pick him? Sebastian walked back and asked the woman if there was someone she wanted us to call. She said her boyfriend was on his way. Great! Let him come right now so I can be relieved of my duty.

Yes, this was a duty for me. The last thing I wanted to do was watch the very thing I had been suppressing in my heart for years, the very thing that I had finally convinced my mind and heart that I didn't want. I don't want this. I don't want this. I don't want this! I kept repeating this over and over again while the woman kept chanting get it out. As the paramedic coached her to push, I began to see this blob emerge. I couldn't believe that I was actually witnessing the birth of a baby. Soon the head was being guided out and then the shoulders, chest, and legs. As the baby began to cry and was placed on the woman's chest, I no longer remembered the conviction I so strongly recited a few moments ago. My tough exterior melted as I watched the new mother guide the baby to her breast. As if on autopilot, the baby began to suckle. Tears ran down the mother's face as the two of them shared the most intimate moment in front of a room of strangers.

As I looked in the eyes of this new mother, what I once saw as a duty I now saw as an honor. The greatest gift any woman can give is life. I walked out of that room transformed. My head spinning as I reflected on what I just experienced. All these years I convinced myself I didn't want something which I now discovered I truly wanted. All I could do was go into my office and cry. I feared that the one thing I longed for, I would never have.

The next morning, I went into work like a zombie. I barely slept the night before. Every time I drifted to dreamland; visions of curly-haired babies danced in front of me. They were calling to me with their tiny arms outstretched but each time I reached for them, they turned into puffs of brown smoke. Each dream turned nightmare jolted me awake. By the time the sun peeked into my bedroom, my breathing was labored, and my body was covered in sweat. It seemed as if the adrenaline rush of my life, as beautiful as it was, had left my body struggling to recover.

My morning shower did nothing to settle my emotions. As I rubbed the soapy washcloth over my taunt, stretchmark free belly, I was once again reminded of how my body had never carried a child. I stood in the shower allowing the hot water to wash away the emotions that leaked from my

38

eyes until the water became cold. One glance in the bathroom mirror told me everything I needed to know about the day. I didn't have the energy to deal with any hotel drama. I just needed to get through my shift without bursting into tears.

"Umm girl…. you must have had a rough night last night! Cuz honey, you look a hot mess."

"Boy bye!"

Sebastian kept running his mouth as I dragged myself into my office. I just wanted to finish some paperwork and then try to find an empty room to sleep in for a few hours. My staff always knew that when I said I was going to a certain room to do an inspection that meant I was going to take a power nap.

I had just turned my computer on when I heard Mrs. Stein talking to Sebastian. I decided to go see how our permanent guest was doing. It had now been two months since Mrs. Stein began her stay with us. She knew all the staff by name and we even had her patio smoke schedule down pat. Like clockwork she would come down at 6:20 am, smoke a cigarette, and then head to the restaurant for breakfast. By 8:10 she was done and back on the patio to read the paper and have another smoke. She would then go to the lobby lounge area and watch "The View" and shout at the commentators as they discussed the latest topics. By 11:00 she was back out at the patio and then upstairs for her nap. She would be back down for a final smoke before heading to the restaurant for dinner.

"Hi, Mrs. Stein. How are you?"

"Oh, I'm hanging in there, sweetie. Just taking one day at a time. You know I am just not the same without my Harry."

You could have fooled me, I thought. Mrs. Stein was always getting packages from Sax and Nordstroms. She never missed her weekly standing nail and hair appointment. Her son sent a car to pick her up and she was out there waiting 10 minutes ahead of time. Don't let her ride be late, or she'd be on her phone cussing Tommy out. Her favorite phrase to shout was, "Where is the damn car?" I admired her for continuing with her life despite losing her husband. I always wanted to ask her when she was moving back home but felt that would be inappropriate to ask. If it was up to her son, Tommy, the house would have already been sold and momma would be in assisted living. I couldn't see her staying in a place like that. She had way too much spunk to be around those folks. For some reason, when I think of places like that, I think of old people who are one step away from diapers and being spoon fed.

"Mrs. Stein, you know you alright with me," I said. "Who knows Mr. Stein might send you a young replacement so you can live that cougar life," I added with a wink.

She cracked up on that one and proceeded to rummage through her purse for a lighter. As she walked towards the patio, I could still hear her chuckling. I wanted to be like her when I grew up- classy and sassy.

Melissa Elizabeth

I started to feel myself getting into that mid-afternoon slump so I decided to head to the kitchen and see if the chef could make my favorite, avocado toast and kale salad. I stopped at the bar and saw Winston, one of the regular bartenders. I knew Happy Hour would be buzzing tonight for Winston drew the ladies like honey draws a bee.

I watched him as he poured a drink for a customer. Winston was a nice-looking guy who was very easy to talk to. However, that's about it when it comes to his good qualities. I don't think there has been a front desk attendant he hasn't slept with except Ethel and Sebastian (and that is only because Winston's not "bi" and he doesn't go for anyone over 40 years of age). He claimed he had standards that he never deviated from. I thought of him as your typical flatliner. Someone who immediately catches your attention but has no ambition to move up in life. He was quite content with bartending and sleeping around.

Winston finished with his customer and headed over to greet me.

"Hey beautiful," he said as he gave me a hug.

Wow, he smelled so delicious (like a mix of bourbon and Versace cologne). I took one final deep whiff before I forced myself to pull away. You could definitely add his looks and scent to his quality meter. The man was pure eye and nose candy for sure!

"How's it going?" I asked as I pretended his scent had no effect on me.

"It's pretty slow."

"Slow huh? You'll eat those words once the HAG floods in," I said with a chuckle.

HAG was our code for the ladies who flocked to Winston during Happy Hour. They were really a sight to see, ranging from young and vibrant to not so young and married. They'd crowd the bar wearing their most revealing outfits hoping to the flavor of the moment to catch his attention. It was a sad sight to see as a woman, but as a hotel employee it was highly entertaining on a slow news day.

"You know it," Winston replied while smiling from ear to ear.

That smile reminded why I'd never been tempted to hop in the sack with him. Aside from the fact that I wasn't into being in anyone's rotation, Winston was missing a tooth right in the front of his mouth which was why Sebastian's nickname for him was snaggle tooth. Winston was sexy when he smirked, but the second he smiled all of that went out of the window for me. I couldn't understand how he caught so many women with that tooth missing, but to each their own, I guess.

I left the bar and headed to the kitchen to get something to eat. I decided that I was going to eat in the restaurant since it was slow instead of going back to my office like I usually did. I needed a break and a change of scenery.

Right when I was about to take a bite into my avocado toast, I saw Sebastian running towards me.

"Maintenance says they need your approval to bust the door guard on room 304," he said almost out of breath.

"Why?"

"They didn't say."

"Tell them I'm on my way," I replied as I handed my food to Winston. "Please put this up for me."

Winston grabbed the plate from me as I quickly made my way to the stairs. I started trying to remember why that room number sounded familiar to me. Of course, I was familiar with all of our room numbers, but something was trying to come to the forefront of my mind. It was as though there was a specific reason I needed to remember this room number. I scanned my memory for all of room assignments from my recent shifts as I sprinted up the steps.

As my foot hit the first step of my last set, I paused in my tracks. That was the guy I checked in last night, the guy I thought was a sugar daddy. He had the eyes of a lost puppy. I immediately didn't like the feeling of this and sprinted even faster up the last few steps. When I got to the floor, I saw Ana outside the door with her cleaning cart and our maintenance guy, Antonio, beside her.

"What's going on?" I asked Ana and Antonio.

"This is the last room I need to clean today. He was supposed to check out this morning, but the guard is still on the door."

"How long have you been trying to get him to open the door?"

"This is the 3rd time I've tried today," Ana replied with a hint of worry in her tone.

"Go ahead and open it," I said to Antonio as Ana and I stepped out of his way.

As he is working on removing the guard I started to panic. What will we find when we enter the room? I called out for the man, but no answer. I knocked on the door asking if anyone was in there. I saw several other guests coming out their rooms and staring so I stopped as not to cause a panic.

Antonio finally got the door guard off and we all just stood there looking at each other. He looked at me and Ana looked at him. I thought to myself this punk is scared. I couldn't stand a man who wouldn't man up when it's necessary. Why is it they love to flex every chance they get, but when you need them to show their manly prowess, they punk out?

I sighed as I realized we would be there all day if I waited for Antonio, so I slowly opened the door and called out for someone… anyone to answer. Please answer, I thought to myself. Realizing my prayer would not be answered, I stepped into the room with Ana and Antonio following closely behind me. As soon as we got past the bathroom, we saw the man lying on the bed. He was face up like he was sleeping on his back. I touched him and he was

44

unresponsive. I immediately knew that he was not going to wake up.

Dread settled upon me as I called down to the front desk and asked them to call 911.

"We have an unresponsive guest in 304," I said into the walkie.

Antonio tapped my shoulder and pointed to the table where I noticed the shopping bag he had with him when he checked in. Next to the bag was a large container of antifreeze. Ana pointed towards the bed he was in and we noticed what appeared to be a note.

My heart sank. I flashed back to that look in his eyes. That was a look of despair, that all hope was gone. It was the look that says there is nothing left to live for. How? Why? What could be so bad that he would resort to this? What would his wife say? His kids? I desperately wanted answers. I reached for the note, but Antonio grabbed my hand and stopped me.

"You better not touch that. The police will probably consider that evidence."

My hand was trembling, but I didn't realize it until Antonio placed both of his large rough hands on my much smaller one to stop the movements. I was numb and didn't know what to do. Antonio finally stepped up.

"Ana, take Morgan downstairs. I will stay here and wait for the authorities to arrive."

I remained silent as Ana took my hand from Antonio and led me out of the room like an obedient child. I was too drained to put up a fight or remind either of them that I was the superior of the three of us. Once again, my emotions were on overdrive. How could it be that within the span of 24 hours I have witnessed the birth of life and the loss of life? All of the efforts I'd made to keep my emotions in check during my shift were quickly becoming null and void. The lump of sadness started to build in the back of my throat before the elevator could reach the lobby. I was determined not to turn into a puddle of tears in front of the hotel staff or guests, so I kept my breathing level and focused on getting out of there as quickly as possible. As soon as I stepped out of the elevator, I heard Winston calling my name.

"Hey, Morgan! What do you want me to do with your food?"

"Box it up," I choked out. "I'm heading home."

Typically, I'd wait for the EMT and Police to arrive, and complete their investigation before I even thought of leaving the hotel premises, but I was at my breaking point. I was strong, but I was human. I knew Sebastian was perfectly capable of handling things whether he liked to admit it or not. I didn't speak to anyone or give any directions. I simply grabbed my purse and coat, stopped to grab my food, and headed for the door. I knew no matter how difficult things became, the hotel would still be standing tomorrow, but if I didn't get home to do so much needed self-care, Morgan would not.

Chapter Three:

A Sexy Friday

I walked into the hotel and immediately knew we were in for a weekend to remember. I saw pre-teen girls and their parents everywhere. I completely forgot we'd booked a group of softball players who were in town for the Little League Softball World Series. I made a mental note to have a brief meeting with housekeeping before they left for the day. All these tween girls meant the pool would be overrun, and towels would be in heavy demand.

I stepped into the office to set my purse down before manning one of the computers at the front desk. There was no way Ethel and Sebastian would be able to handle all of the registrations alone.

The first family I checked in had a set of twin girls who looked so much a like I couldn't figure out how anyone told them apart. From their matching outfits and ponytails, to the matching mole right below their left ears, the girls were dead ringers for one another. I smiled broadly as the girls asked if the pool was open. I could tell it wasn't planned but they asked the question at the exact same time.

When I confirmed it was, a sneaky look crossed both of their faces.

I looked at the parents as said, "The girls will need to be accompanied when they go to the pool."

"Oh they're 12. They should be fine on their own," the mother replied.

"Well, it's hotel policy that no one under the age if 18 is left alone in the pool when we have a group of minors staying in the hotel. It's to ensure their safety," I lied.

"Is there something we need to know?" their father asked.

I could instantly see his chest swell as though he could chest bump a threat into submission. I regretted my choice of words, but quickly smiled as I spout out another lie. "Years ago, we heard of a story of teens playing around in a hotel pool without supervision. One of the children bumped their head and nearly drowned. We instituted our policy immediately after hearing the story. We take the safety of all our guests very seriously."

Both the mom and dad seemed to relax upon hearing my response. The girls however, seemed upset I'd ruined their plans. I didn't care though. I was not about to have another weekend of pool pranks like we did when the baseball team stayed at the hotel. They poured Kool-Aid packets into the pool turning the water bright red. I didn't have time for the shenanigans of bored kids.

I finished checking the family in and called Juanita, one of our housekeepers, on the radio.

"Yes, Ms. Morgan?" Jaunita replied.

"I need you to take extra towels to room 518. And make a note to leave extra towels when the room is cleaned tomorrow. They have twin daughters who will need the extra towels for the pool."

"What!?" Juanita yelled into the radio.

I yanked the radio away from my face surprised by how loud her voice was. I glanced up to see if anyone else heard her. The way everyone was staring at me told me my answer.

"What was that Juanita?" I said into the radio.

"I'm sorry Ms. Morgan. I thought I saw something, but I was mistaken. I'll take the towels right now."

I didn't even bother responding. Just sat the radio down and started helping the next family check in.

An hour later, we had the lobby cleared and Sebastian happily joined me in the office so we both could rest our feet.

"Girl, what was Juanita yelling about?"

"I have no idea. I wasn't about to ask her to explain because you know there's no telling what will come out of her mouth."

Sebastian and I both laughed know what I said was true. Juanita had the reputation for saying exactly what she was thinking which is why we tried to keep her interactions with guests to a minimum. Before I could even say another word, Ethel rushed into the office.

"Morgan, I need you to come up front. A guest is asking to speak to you."

"Who is it?"

"The couple with the twins."

"I swear those girls better not have done anything. They just got here," I warned as I stood to follow Ethel back to the front desk.

When I saw the parents' faces, I could see anger radiating from both of them. "Hello again," I said with a smile. "How may I help you?"

"First, we never got those extra towels you promised. Second, you can tell that pervert not to watch porn in a public place," the mother yelled.

"Excuse me?"

"There is a man in your business center watching porn. We could see his screen when we walked by the window," the father stated.

"Oh, I know no one is crazy enough to do that here," I stated as I hurried towards the business center. The last thing I needed was for some child to stumble upon something their eyes had no business seeing. That type of publicity would be terrible for the hotel. I rounded the corner and barged into the business center. I saw one man sitting there quietly playing chess.

"Excuse me Sir," I said as I glanced around the room to see if any of the other monitors were on. They were not. "Was anyone else in here with you this afternoon?"

"No. I haven't been here long though. Are you looking for someone?"

"No. I received a complaint, but it must have been a false alarm. I'll let you get back to your game."

I didn't wait for a response. I closed the door and breathed a sigh of relief. When I got back to the front desk, I informed the couple I only saw one man in the room and he was playing chess not watching porn.

"I know porn when I see it," the mother yelled. "I ain't never seen tits and ass in no chess game."

Ethel gasped loudly and Sebastian stifled a laugh. I didn't have time for Ethel and her strict Christian views or Sebastian and his love for drama, so I ignored them both.

"Well, I can only tell you what I saw. The man was playing chess."

"Well, we know what we saw and I'm tell you right now, if that man so much as looks at my wife or my daughters, you better call the police because I'm going to kill him," the father said before grabbing his wife's arm and walking away.

"Chile... Daddy say he ain't playing no games about his tuhday!" Sebastian said as soon as the couple was out of earshot.

"I can't believe people actually talk like that in public," Ethel said grabbing her chest as though she was mortified.

"Loosen up Church Lady," Sebastian teased. "Everybody ain't saved."

"I know that! That's the problem," Ethel said as she stormed off.

"Why do you have to get her riled up?" I asked Sebastian. "You know how she is."

"Well, she needs to loosen up. We're all too grown for her to be acting all offended by words like tits and ass. Hell, if she gave somebody some of either one of those, she'd stop being so uptight."

"Dainel!"

"What? Don't act so surprised. You know who you work with."

Before I could even respond, Ethel came running back up to the front desk. "Ms. Morgan, he is in there watching porn."

This time, I tip toed my way to the business center. I didn't want the click clack of my heels to let him know I was coming. I slowly peeked my head around the corner and sure enough, the man was clicking between screens. One second he was pretending to play chess, the next he was watching porn. I rushed to the door and flung it open.

"Sir, that is inappropriate to watch on a public computer. Anyone walking by can see your screen from the window. If this happens again, I will have to ask you to leave."

"It won't happen again," the man said turning to look at me with the most remorseful expression. His eyes were large blue pools that women probably got lost in. Hell, had I not just seen him watching porn in public, I would probably consider him handsome. Knowing what I knew about him ruined any chance of attraction.

I shut the door and returned to the front desk.

"Was he really watching porn?" Sebastian asked.

"Yes! Can you believe that?"

"No. Why can't he just be like a regular man and watch it on his phone in his room?"

I decided to ignore Sebastian's regular man comment. "What room is he staying in?" I asked Ethel.

She shook her head. "I don't know. I didn't check him in.

"Sebastian, go check on him and see if you recognize him. I want to make sure we keep an eye on him."

Sebastian left and quickly returned. "I've never seen him before. He must have checked in with day shift."

"Okay. Just go check on him periodically to make sure he doesn't watch anything else inappropriate in there. I'm going to take a break. Oh, and call Juanita and remind her to take the towels to 518," I said over my shoulder.

Melissa Elizabeth

An hour later, I casually stroll pass the business center on my way back to the front desk. I'd taken a power nap and finally felt ready to tackle my reports. I stopped in my tracks as soon as I could peek into the business center window. The man was still there, but now he wasn't alone. There was a woman sitting next to him. Both of their chairs were turned slightly towards one another. His eyes were closed and hers were locked on the computer screen. I couldn't see exactly what they were doing, but I could see enough to figure it out.

I ducked down and quietly crossed beneath the window. I got to the front desk and went straight to the phone. I called the police and asked them to quickly send officers to help us evict a couple performing a sex act in public. When I hung up the phone, Ethel and Sebastian were both staring at me with their mouths hanging open.

"Girl, where is this couple? I need to see this!" Sebastian said excitedly as he tried to rush past me.

"Oh no you don't." I grabbed his arm preventing him from leaving. "We're all gonna wait right here for the police."

It took the police less than ten minutes to arrive. Two officers followed me to the business center where the couple had progressed from pleasuring each other by hand to full blown intercourse. The police interrupted their interlude and brought the pair to my office so that I could gather their information. I needed to make sure their names were in the system so that they'd been banned from staying at the hotel ever again.

Imagine my shock to learn the guy wasn't even a guest. He was a local who claimed our night auditor frequently allowed him to use the business center when his internet was out at home. He said he'd been coming to our hotel for over a year, but always at night. That explained why he was so comfortable watching porn in there.

His female companion turned out to be one of the mothers from the softball team. Apparently, she'd been so turned on when she saw him watching porn that she'd accepted his invitation to join him. Both were arrested and barred from ever staying at the hotel again. The woman's daughter nearly died from embarrassment when she learned she would have to stay in her coach's custody until they returned home due to her mother's arrest. The last words the daughter yelled before her coach hauled her into the elevator were, "I hope it was worth it because I'm calling Dad right now!"

By the time we got the lobby settled again, it was almost time to go home. I noticed Ethel was getting off the elevator. With all the commotion, I didn't even notice her leave.

"Where are you coming from?"

"Room 518. Jaunita never took them the towels."

"What? Why not? What time did she leave?"

"At 6pm. After her las show ended."

"Last show?" Now I was confused.

"Yes," Sebastian cut in. "Apparently that heifer was upstairs watching Telemundo TV instead of working. We've been getting calls left and right for stuff she should have done long before she left."

"Oh, that's definitely going to be a write-up. Write a statement for me so I can add it to her file. We have too much guest drama to be dealing with lazy staff," I said before grabbing my coat and purse to leave. Technically I still had another hour to go, but I was over it. Seeing strangers have sex made me feel like I needed a shower!

Chapter Four:

The Battle Royal

"Sebastian, you won't believe this!"

Sebastian came running into my office sighing, "What now?"

I proceeded to tell him that our idiot boss decided to book two major events that weekend. Generally, this wouldn't be a problem. However, these types of events should never occur simultaneously at the same hotel.

"Your boss booked a Psychic Convention and a retreat sponsored by the Zion Holiness Pentecostal Kingdom Church," I said as laughter poured from the pit of my belly.

"Umm, this should be interesting," smirked Sebastian as he headed out front.

Following behind him, I informed him that Ethel and Marley Rain were working the desk with him the whole weekend. I knew that would get his attention.

"Awwww Lord! Are you kidding me?"

I shook my head, but I had to admit I was thoroughly enjoying his reaction. You see, just like the convention and retreat were like a cold and warm front colliding to cause violent storms with the potential to leave disasters and trauma in their wake, so were Ethel and Marley Rain.

Ethel was our resident church lady whom we blatantly referred to as such when we weren't calling her our church mother. Marley Rain, a new hire, was your typical BoHo chick who could be described as being extremely YOGA-fied and totally ZEN-tastic. She was constantly talking about something called mindfulness. Sebastian liked to say she was more mindless than mindful. The ladies were like oil and water. Ethel found Marley irritating, and Marley found Ethel stubborn and narrow-minded. The combination of the four entities was a sure-fire recipe for a spark-filled weekend! I was sure I'd be spending my time trying to keep Ethel out of the retreat and Marley out of the convention.

I told Sebastian that I hoped he was ready for this and proceeded to find Jacque our Director of Sales and Catering who handled all our events. I discovered him in our Asbury Room which was our biggest ballroom. Our six conference and meeting rooms at the hotel were named after some of the state beaches. We had the Asbury, Seaside, Belmar, Stone Harbor, Avalon, and Manasquan. I always wondered what the inspiration was behind the names of hotel ballrooms. If I ever got up enough nerve to have my own Bed and Breakfast my rooms would be named after iconic movie stars like the Cecily Chamber, the

Denzel Digs, and the Ruby Dee Rotunda, a round room in the center of the building that would cause all who saw it to stop and stare.

I often say I should be taking all that I have learned from being in the hotel industry to go in business for myself. Even during a time of AirBnB, I still believed there were many who seek after the intimate service of a B&B.

Jacque, with his binder in hand, had just finished meeting with our event staff. This included the catering staff, the maintenance crew, housekeeping, and our multimedia team. As soon as he saw me, he ran over to me screaming, "Morgan, I am so glad you are here. I was just about to come see you."

"Hey Jacque. How are things going? We all set for our events this weekend?"

"We have a problem. The convention promoters just informed me that the electronic screen they were to have here yesterday is stuck in New York and won't be here until late this afternoon. How are we to get this thing set up before the banquet tonight?"

After asking him a few more inquiring questions we decided that since the screen wasn't needed until the following morning, we would have the team set it up after the banquet which was scheduled to end at 10 pm.

Jacque rolled his eyes knowing that the team was not going to like that. One thing I could say about Jacque was that he could put such a positive spin on anything that he has fired people and they walked away smiling. He was one of the few folks I did not have to constantly follow behind to ensure that things were done properly. He was such a perfectionist that I knew things would get done and get done right. His motto is, "Honey, if I am runnin' things its gonna be run right!" I have watched him turn our ballrooms from enchanted gardens to disco halls. He was one of the main reasons we have so many events at our hotel. We have established a great reputation as an event venue mainly because of Jacque.

I looked at him and said, "Chile, that is the least of your worries."

"Hmmm, don't I know it. I am just fixing the ring for this boxing match. You're the one who's gotta referee it."

We laughed and hugged each other. As I headed back to the lobby, I saw Ms. Stein leaving the restaurant. She was still hanging in here. She was entering into her sixth month with us. I usually hated long term guests, but she was an exception. I have enjoyed our conversations and her unusual perception of life. I could tell she'd been through a lot more than what she let on, but you would never know it by looking at her. Even if she was just going to pick up a USA Today from the lobby she was still dressed to the nines. Not a hair out of place and dressed like she was headed to the synagogue.

Regardless of how well her exterior was put together, there was a look that escaped her when she was deep in conversation. Perhaps she felt comfortable talking to me, or maybe her old age was causing her rock-hard persona to slip… I couldn't tell which one it was. Yet, I knew there was more to the older woman than she cared to show. It was is if she'd perfected the act of looking okay while her world was on fire around her. It took a perfectly crafted polished exterior to recognize it in someone else. If there was one thing I had, it was a well put together exterior.

Suddenly, I saw Ms. Stein stop for a minute and grab her hip. Her unusual show vulnerability snapped me out of my revelry. I rushed to her.

"Are you okay?" I asked as I reached her side.

"Awww… I'm fine, Honey," she said as she smiled through her discomfort. "You know Arthur wants to come around every now and then. He just needs to leave us seniors alone."

I chuckled. My grandmother used to refer to her arthritis as Arthur too. I wrapped my arm around her and assisted her to the chair located by the refreshment area. She reminded me of my grandmother. Whenever I would stop by and see her, I had to make sure I didn't come empty handed. She loved caramel hard candies, RC Cola, and pretzel sticks. I would be chewed out if I also didn't have a tube of Bengay in the bag. We always knew when her arthritis was acting up by the smell of her home. Sometimes we had to open all the windows for the "smell of the Gay" was so strong. Back in the day that is what the old folks used for "Arthur" religiously.

Once I got her settled, I sat beside her and told her, "He better go to his other chick cause you ain't in the mood to be touched today."

"What?" Ms. Stein looked at me with total confusion.

"That's what my grandmother used to say when "Author" tried to bother her."

Ms. Stein threw her head back and laughed the loudest, heartiest laugh I ever heard come out of her. The sound was like music to my ears. It took her a moment to finally calm down after the belly laugh. When she regained her composure, she grabbed my hand. I looked at her beautifully manicured shriveled up hand and placed my hand on top of it. For the first time I felt how thin and fragile it was. I was surprised to notice that the hand tremors were not occurring.

Ms. Stein turned to me and shared a story of when she was young. She told me how she had a dear friend that she met one day on the subway. They used to take the same train into the city every morning and began to talk. They would look for each other on the platform so they could board the same car. Their conversation grew until an hour train ride felt like ten minutes. One day, they decided to stay in the city after work and grab a bite to eat. That led to a thirty-year friendship. She described how she was introduced to Harlem through this friend. Her friend knew the owner of a club in Harlem who would always let them in even though they were underaged.

I watched her as she recounted this story. As she talked, you could tell she loved that time in her life. The whole time she never let go of my hand. She gently held it as if she was with her friend again… as if I was her friend and they were together one more time. This walk down memory lane had put her into a trance like state – like she was back there again.

Her face then took a dark turn. She shared that all that had changed after the Harlem Riot of 1968. The owner didn't want any trouble and asked her friend not to bring Ms. Stein around anymore. Her parents found out where she was hanging out and forbade her to go back to Harlem. She said it took her 20 years before she returned to Harlem.

When she came out of her trance like state, she looked over at me and just stared. After a few seconds she said, "You remind me of her. She was so pretty and had soft eyes like you." She then took her hand and gently rubbed it across my cheek.

I just sat there in silence. Normally I don't like anyone touching my face let alone getting close to it, but I didn't want to ruin this moment for her. So, I just sat there and listened. She then got up and gave me a hug and walked away. As she walked away, she yelled, "Looks like y'all got a lot going on this weekend."

Right then and there I assured myself that I was going to make it my mission to find out who the real Margaret Stein was. But first, I needed to get back to the front desk before

Sebastian sent out a search party. He hated when I disappeared too long.

As I headed to the front, I saw a charter bus outside. Along the side of the bus, I saw in big letters the words, **Zion Holiness Pentecostal Kingdom Church**. Right next to the words there was a picture of an older gentleman who was grinning from ear to ear with his arms stretched out like he wanted to hug someone. I did a double take. Wass that a gold tooth? I read the name underneath the picture, Reverend TK Stokes. I guessed our retreat folks had arrived.

I turned towards the lobby and saw Sebastian, Ethel, and Marley diligently checking in our lobby full of guests. The lobby had become a sea of women all wearing long skirts and shirts with the ZHPKC logo on them. As I got to the desk Sebastian mumbled under his breathe, "Oh, good to see you. You know we serve an on-time God."

Ethel must have heard him because she cosigned with, "Amen and Hallelujah."

I ignored Sebastian's shade and Ethel's cluelessness and headed to help Marley who looked like a deer in headlights. Her guest was asking a ton of questions and she looked as nervous as a teenager taking their driver's test. Marley saw me coming and practically shove me towards the lady. I greeted her and asked if there was anything else she needed.

"I am Apostle Bettina Stokes, the First Lady of Zion Holiness Pentecostal Kingdom Church," she said as if her name and title meant something to me. "I need a suite with a king bed, but this young lady is telling me you do not have any available."

The way she said young lady clearly revealed her judgement of Marley which wasn't sitting well with me, but I wasn't going to let her ruffle my feathers. I checked the reservation. It clearly showed a standard room with two double beds. She probably just recently came into a little extra money and wanted to upgrade. She couldn't have her congregates see her in a regular room if she could help it. It was all about keeping up the image. I started to pretend we didn't have any just to embarrass her as payback for judging my staff, but I resisted the urge. After a few clicks of the mouse, I spoke to her again.

"Marley is correct, we were fully booked this weekend, but we had a cancellation just a moment ago. I've updated your reservation."

She thanked me and testified about how good God was as I prepared her room keys. Sebastian and I gave each other the "please don't start stomping and shouting in our lobby" look. Marley, trying to make amends, asked Apostle Stokes if she wanted us to get someone to take her bags up to her room.

Apostle looked at Marley like she was crazy and said, "No thank you dear." She turned and rolled her eyes annoyed that Marley didn't understand that she would never let a stranger touch her bags. "Sister Mattie, get my bags please," Apostle demanded as she walked towards the elevator. She didn't even bother to make eye contact with the person she was ordering around. Her arrogance was disgusting but not surprising. I've seen my share of "church leaders" act like their members were their personal valets.

Marley looked at me with the "what did I do" look. I just shrugged my shoulders to let her know it was okay and not to let it get to her. After about thirty minutes we could finally see our lobby again. The women were all checked in and headed to their rooms to prepare for the evening service scheduled for 7 pm.

"I'm going to take my break before the convention crew arrive," Sebastian announced before anyone else could leave.

"Okay," I responded.

He headed toward the restaurant but bolted back and grabbed me. He pulled me to the front door.

"Girl, you see this." He pointed to the church bus. "You know who that is don't you?"

"No, who is he?"

"He don't look familiar to you?" Sebastian asked.

"No," I say impatiently.

"That's our regular, Teddy Kinard!"

"What!" I yelled before clasping my hand over my mouth. I couldn't believe it. I didn't recognize him all suited up on the bus. He'd been staying at the hotel often, but he always wore sweats and a baseball cap. We never understood why he came in so often, sometimes not even staying the whole night. Sebastian told me that one-time housekeeping found cocaine in his room.

"Are you sure, Sebastian? I didn't think Teddy had a gold tooth."

"Boo, that is him! Trust me. I've gotten more than one good look at him, if you know what I mean," He winked before skipping off acting like he discovered gold or something.

"What?!" I yelled again. "Sebastian, what are you saying?" I half yelled; half whispered.

"I'm not saying anything other than this may be the most entertaining weekend we've ever had," he said as he kept walking.

I rubbed my temples. The thought of what Sebastian could be planning was too much for me to take on. He could be real messy when he wanted to be. If he had the low-down on Teddy, he was definitely going to use the information to his advantage. And if the First Lady was anywhere near as arrogant as I believed her to be, there were going to be more fireworks than the 4th of July.

I decided to let Sebastian enjoy his break instead of pestering him for more information like I wanted to. I went to check the conference rooms to ensure they were ready for the evening. Upon finding them all set up and ready to go, I headed back to my office to handle paperwork until the next big round of guests arrived.

After a couple hours I came out my office to see guests starting to check in for the Psychic Convention. I heard Sebastian's crazy self say, "You are in room 415 but I'm sure you already knew that." He was a mess. When he was done, he came over to me and asked if I thought they could read him. He was so scared that one of them was going to tell him they heard his dead grandmother speaking to them or tell him something bad, like he was going to die in a car accident.

"Sebastian don't be silly. You watch too much TV!" Marley told him. "That's not what they do."

"It's all demonic if you ask me," Ethel chimed in.

"Nobody asked you," Marley retorted.

"Little girl, you really want me to come out my religion don't you," Ethel screamed shoving her finger in Marley's face. What happened to our sweet Ethel?

I immediately stepped in between them and stated the obvious, "I see somebody wants to lose their job tonight."

Ethel gave me a harsh look but backed off. Lord knows I needed Apostle to come down here and pray over this front desk. But then again, if her husband was Teddy, our regular, maybe not.

Uh oh, I must have talked her up because as soon as the elevator dinged, I looked up to see her. Apostle Stokes came charging towards the front desk pointed back at the marquee located by the front door.

"Why wasn't I told there was going to be a Psychic Convention here this weekend? I should have been informed these spirits and demons would be all up in this building. We're going to need to pray and anoint this area. Let me go get my intercessors and my holy oil." She marched off like she was ready for battle.

I didn't bother to tell her that much worse things go on in a hotel on a daily basis. She was acting like folks didn't go to hotels to fornicate, use drugs, commit adultery, and more. There were probably more spirits in any hotel on any given day than what the convention could bring. Hotels are, by nature, a place where people go to do things they may not be able to do at home for any number of reasons, but again, I wouldn't dare tell Apostle that.

Twenty minutes later we had women scattered all throughout the lobby and lower level where the conference rooms were located. They were whispering prayers and finger flinging oil all over the place. Sebastian looked at me with his head cocked to the side and his hand on his hip. I knew he was asking me if I was really going to let the ladies keep up with their shenanigans. Those who know me know I hate confrontation, so I figured as long as the convention hadn't started it was okay. Just as I thought the women weren't harming anyone, I heard Jacque screaming.

"Y'all better stop flinging that oil around these plates and silverware."

I immediately rushed towards the sound of his voice. I needed to get to him before he put the women out of his ballroom. I got there just in time to grab his arm before he yelled out something crazy.

"Jacque, please ignore them. They aren't hurting anyone."

"Not hurting anyone? Don't you know that oil will stain my fine linens? I'm not letting them ruin my reputation with their foolishness."

"Please Jacque…."

"Fine!" He stated realizing I was literally begging him. "If there is one stain on my tablecloths, you better be ready to sign off on my purchase order to replace them."

Jacque stormed off leaving me standing there silently thanking God one small crisis had been avoided. I wasn't delusional though. I knew Jacque was the least of my worries. It was almost time for the banquet and church service to begin. The convention attendees were having to walk past the intercessors in the hallway to get into the banquet hall. Every time the elevator door opened, they would jump into action-praying in tongues and shouting out scriptures. It got so bad that the promoters asked them to stop upon which they dosed them with holy oil and tried to lay hands on them.

I saw one of the promoters heading towards me and instantly knew he was on his way to complain. I smiled and said, "I see what's going on. I'll speak to them at once."

Though he was still unhappy, he stepped to the side so that I could go speak to the women praying.

"Ladies," I began in the sweetest voice I could muster out, "The Lord is omnipresent and omnipotent. I am sure he can hear you if you pray inside of the conference room. It has already been set up for your service."

"But Apostle told us to stand out here and cast the demons out as soon as they stepped off of the elevator."

I felt my nerves wearing thin. It was one thing to be disturbing my peace, but I would not let them disrespect our other guests. "I'm sure Apostle will understand the need to do everything in decency and order. Your retreat is scheduled to be held inside the conference room, not in our hallway."

I could tell the women were not too please with my decency and order comment, but they did not protest. They resumed speaking in tongues as they walked towards the conference room. One of the ladies made sure to speak in English when she yelled over her shoulder, "I'd rather be inside listening to Rev. Stokes preach than out here congregating with these devils anyway."

I should have been annoyed by her comment, but I wasn't. I rushed to go find Sebastian. I knew he'd enjoy spying on the "Rev" as much as I would. Sebastian was my certified partner in being messy at work.

Melissa Elizabeth

When I reached Sebastian, I didn't bother saying a word. I just grabbed his hand and pulled him towards the conference room.

"Why are you pulling me? You know bunion can't handle all this fast walking."

I didn't reply. I just pulled him into the conference room. As we took our positions at the back of the room, we could see Rev. Stokes walking to the podium. He looked so stoic and dignified up there. After a few customary Praise the Lords and God is Goods he proceeded to welcome all the ladies to the retreat and honored his wife and the women's ministry for all their hard work in putting the retreat together. He then shared with the audience that he had a word from the Lord. He titled his message, 'A Wolf in Sheep's Clothing'. Sebastian and I immediately gave each other a knowing look. That was the pot calling the kettle black, but we both remained silent as we listened to him tell the people what he should have been saying to himself.

Rev. Stokes took his time detailing how we often disguise who we really are because of the strongholds that we have not let go of in our life. He proclaimed that we have to have faith and trust in God, and that by doing so, God would be able to break the chains of bondage that are stopping us from walking in the full purpose that He has for us. He started to get excited when talking about how God knows and sees and wants to help us overcome our sin and transgressions. God doesn't need hocus pocus magic or spells to undercover what we are truly hiding.

When he said that, I knew he was throwing shade at the convention attendees. I rolled by eyes at the hypocrisy of his words, but his congregates were eating it all up.

Within fifteen minutes he had people running around the room shouting, dancing, and falling out. Women were running to the altar dropping twenty-dollar bills at his feet. The ushers would periodically come and place the bills in a basket. Sebastian whispered to me, "I betcha I know what he's gonna use that money for." He then proceeded to hold down one nostril with his finger while sniffing hard with the other nostril. I pushed him and looked to make sure no one saw or heard him. One usher saw us laughing and immediately shot us this evil look. I pushed Sebastian again as if to say we better get out of there.

Sebastian went towards the door shouting and stomping like he had the Holy Ghost. We bust through the door cracking up. I couldn't believe what I just saw. I told Sebastian that Rev. Stokes sure was charismatic and was probably preaching more to himself than the congregation.

"Oh he's charismatic alright," Sebastian replied.

"There you go again. If you know more about him, just go ahead and spit it out already."

Sebastian stopped walking and turned to face me with a devilish grin. "I already spit 'it' out last week."

I clasped my hand over my mouth trying to stifle a scream! "No you didn't! You and Teddy… I mean Rev. Stokes? I thought you had a no guest rule."

"I broke my rule, and for he was packing, it was worth it," Sebastian said still smiling.

I'm not one to judge what anyone does in their private time, but I've never been one to want the details of what goes on in another person's bedroom. I never understood why women would want to share the details of their intimate life with another woman who could possibly become a little too intrigued about what she heard. That being said, Sebastian's remark would have typically been the end of the conversation, but I had to know more.

I leaned in closer to Sebastian so that no one else could hear me. "You don't feel bad now that you know he's married?"

Sebastian's face went from jovial to stone cold serious. "Listen, I am a single man who enjoys sleeping with men. If one of those men has a wife, that's his problem. I didn't make a vow to be faithful to anyone."

"Did you at least use protection so he doesn't take anything back home to his wife?"

This time, I could tell I struck a nerve. Sebastian narrowed his eyes and looked at me like he wanted to run through me. "No! I used protection so that he wouldn't give anything to ME! It's not my job to protect either one of them. I protect myself because whether you or society want to admit it, there are married men who like to creep with gay men when they get bored with bland missionary sex at home. Those same men will hop from bed to bed afraid they'll catch feelings if they stick with one person. That's how the diseases get passed around. And for the record, just because I'm gay, that doesn't mean I have AIDS!"

His voice was now elevated. "Sebastian, I'm sorry. I wasn't saying you did. You know I love you. I could never think that about you."

"Oh, you thought it. I just never thought you'd actually say it to my face," Sebastian replied with tears welling in his eyes. I could tell I'd hurt him. He turned and began to walk away, and I knew it was to stop me from seeing him cry.

"Sebastian, please don't go. I didn't mean it like that." I pleaded but did not follow him. I knew I needed to give him space. I also needed to check on the convention. Maybe if I give him a second to pull himself together, he would be willing to listen to my apology. I needed the time to think about what he said anyway. I knew I wasn't a bigot, but did I really have unconscious biases towards gay men? Now I felt my own emotions welling up. I forced the thoughts from my mind so that guests wouldn't find me standing in the hallway crying.

I went back into work mode and poked my head into the banquet. Everyone was seated and eating. It was certainly a different vibe from next door and every now and then you could hear Rev. Stokes' hallelujahs. I went over to our sound guy and asked him to turn the dining music up a little bit more, in hopes of drowning out the church service next door. I had to give it to the convention attendees. They handled themselves well considering how disruptive the retreat had been.

The remainder of evening went smoothly. Sebastian avoided me, which was painful, but I understood his need for space. I knew in time he'd forgive me.

Sunday afternoon, as both the convention and retreat were closing, I stepped into the conference room to make sure they hadn't left any damage behind. I found Apostle Stokes sitting alone in the room. My entrance caused her to stop her silent prayer and look in my direction.

"I apologize. I didn't realize you were in there," I said as I prepared to quickly exit the room.

"It's okay," she said. "I was just thanking God for another successful retreat."

I noticed her countenance was completely different. The arrogance and superiority complex were gone. Instead, I saw glimpses of a real woman whose brokenness resembled my own. Her shoulders were slouched and the lines around her eyes told me everything I needed to know. She wasn't thanking God when I interrupted her. She was releasing all of her burdens to Him.

"Are you sure you're okay, Apostle?"

She looked up and me and gave me a weak smile before responding. "There's nothing God can't handle. He has a plan for everything, even the things that catch us by surprise."

I wasn't sure what she was hinting at, so I changed the subject. "I got to hear Rev. Stokes' message on the first night of the retreat. It was really good."

"Yes, he has always been a gifted preacher. The gifts and the callings of the Lord are without repentance."

"Huh?" I didn't mean for the sound to slip out, but she was being so vulnerable that I let my guard down. It slipped out before I could censor myself.

"It just means God doesn't take gifts away from His people because of our sins. He is gracious towards us even when we don't deserve it."

"I know that to be true," I said, not know what else to say.

"I hope you also know it's not too late for you to use your gifts," she said taking me completely by surprise. "Don't look so surprised. The Holy Spirit showed me some things about you. You got stuck here in this hotel, but you are destined for so much more. Don't let fear keep you here."

I was so shocked by the accuracy of her statement. How could this stranger know anything about me? Maybe she should be next door with the psychic because she just read me better than any phony Ms. Cleo ever could.

She spoke up as though she was reading my thoughts. "No, I'm not a psychic. It's the same gift though. We just use it differently. I use mine for the glory of God. They use theirs for the devil."

I stood silently watching this woman who had completely shocked me. Now that her onlookers were gone, she was a different person. She was kind and humble… real. I hated what I knew about her husband even more now. This woman didn't deserve what he was doing to her. I wondered why God hadn't shown her what he was doing.

As if she read my mind she commented, "God showed me what my husband is years ago. I came to this hotel to see who he does it with. I wasn't shocked when I saw the young man behind your front desk. He's his type."

This time my mouth flew open. I was standing there in total bewilderment as this woman told me she knew her husband slept with men. I couldn't understand why a woman would choose to stay married to a gay man, and why she would agree to keep up his public hypocrisy.

"My husband and I haven't been intimate in years. I never really believed he was into me, but our families insisted we get married. Year one, when it became evident he wasn't interested in having sex with me, I prayed God would never cause our few sexual encounters to result in children. I knew it was my job to cover him in prayer, and I accepted the call, but I did not want to raise children with him. God honored my prayer and I honored my commitment to be my husband's intercessor. He's called to preach the word of God, but he has flaws like everyone else. There are no big sins or small sins Morgan. They all stink in God's nostrils."

"But why are you telling me all this? You don't know me from a can of paint."

"I see a little of myself in you. You're holding your breath waiting for the perfect situation to come before you go after what you want. You're gifted Morgan. You don't need a man or a child to validate you. Go after what you want while you're young."

I scoffed at the young comment. "I don't know about that young part."

"Compared to me, you are young. Create the life you see in your dreams. Trust God enough to pursue what you really want."

I didn't realize I was crying until I felt the cold wet tear drop on my shirt. I thought Apostle Stokes was ridiculous when I first met her. Now I see there is so much more to her than what meets the eye. She stood and handed me a tissue to wipe my tears before stepping back to give me a final word of advice.

"God loves you Morgan. Don't you ever forget that. Take some time to get to know Him better so that He can reveal His plans for your life. If you don't remember anything I said to you today, remember this. Everyone has a cross to carry. Some of us carry it better than others, but we all have one. Never feel down about the weight of your cross."

With that, she turned and walked out of the conference room. I was stunned at everything that transpired in such a short period of time. She was practically a stranger, yet she was completely vulnerable with me. She told me things I doubted many people knew. But why? Why would she open up to me? How did she know I wouldn't run and blab all of her business to anyone who would listen? Another errant tear gave me my answer. She knew I would keep her secrets because I knew she knew mine as well. What we shared was a sacred moment and I would never betray her confidence.

I wiped my face a final time and pulled my cell phone from my pocket to use the camera as a mirror. Once I was comfortable with my appearance, I exited the conference room. What I saw next stopped me dead in my tracks.

On the large electronic screen we'd set up for the Psychic Convention, were the words:

Your husband is gay, and he uses cocaine to forget how much he hates himself.

Apostle Stokes looked around to see if anyone had seen the words on the screen. There were only convention attendees in sight. She fixed her eyes on one of the attendees. I knew a fight was about to break out, so I hurried to her side to usher her away from the area. When I reached her side, the arrogant woman I met upon her arrival had returned.

"Get your hands off of me. You're probably in on these lies that devil put up on that screen," she yelled at me.

I stepped back wondering where the kind woman I spoke to a moment ago went. I opened my mouth to refute her charges, but the head psychic stepped up and spoke for me.

"Ms. Morgan had nothing to do with your reading."

"Reading!" Apostle Stokes looked as if she had smoke coming from her ears. "I never participated in your demonic readings."

"That screen performs psychic readings through the use of artificial intelligence. It's the new wave in psychic technology. You were so busy trying to spy on us that you stood too close to it and it gave you a reading."

I stood there barely able to stifle my laugh. This whole time I was commending the psychics for not responding to the church members' foolishness, and they were silently waiting for their chance to exact their revenge. Apostle Stokes was so shocked by what was happening that she fainted on the spot. No one rushed to her aide. Everyone realized she was just trying to shift their attention away from the screen. I looked at the head psychic and he smiled at me and mouthed, "check mate."

Chapter Five:

Sunday Shenanigans

My mom had been trying to get me to come over for Sunday brunch for the longest. I kept putting it off. I work most Sundays, and when I do get a Sunday off, all I want to do is sleep and binge watch movies. Besides, most black families have Sunday dinner not Sunday brunch. Growing up, half my friends didn't even know what a brunch was until they were invited to our house for one.

I don't recall our Sunday dinner tables looking like the one from the movie Soul Food. You know that table filled up with ham, greens, macaroni and cheese, cornbread, sweet potatoes, fried chicken, and green beans. Mom never got the hang of southern cooking. She is a northerner through and through. Now Dad on the other hand was born and raised in the South. I think when he met Mom, he had to accept the fact that he'd have to wait till he visits his hometown to get southern cooking. Furthermore, my mom is not the best cook, so I think it was just easier for her to make brunch food and still be in compliance with following the black family tradition of big meals on

Sundays. I mean really, who can mess up eggs, bacon, pancakes, and fried apples. So, in our house we had big Sunday brunches at 12:30 pm sharp and ate what was left over for dinner.

I decided to sacrifice my free Sunday and join the family for brunch. I figured it would get my mom off my back as well as have some food to take to lunch tomorrow since I hadn't been grocery shopping in three weeks.

I rolled out of bed and was just about to hop in the shower when my phone rang. I thought about ignoring it but decided to answer it, in case it was my mom calling asking me to stop at the store before I got to her house. I looked down and saw that it wasn't Mom, but work. I reluctantly answered it. It was Antonio, the head of our maintenance department. He was fussing because Mario, the new guy we hired, arrived two hours late for his shift. I explained to Antonio that he knew what procedures to follow. He needed to fill out a policy violation report and place it in my box. I informed him that I would handle it the following day when I returned to work. Antonio had been on me about Mario since we hired him. I knew the kid was a little lazy, but I asked Antonio to just give him some time to adjust to the expectations of this new job. Mario seemed like a good kid and I just wanted to give him a chance. Antonio told me, "That's like trying to squeeze lemon juice out of a lime."

I hung up the phone and let out a scream. For once I would like to not be bothered with work on my day off. I took a quick shower and start to get dressed. Afterwards, I had a hard time deciding what to wear. I have never really been satisfied with my body. Since I was a little girl, I have always been what my mom calls "big boned." I was always much taller and fuller figured for my age. As a full-grown woman, I remained taller than the average woman and had curves that could stop traffic. While I love my curves, I wish I had less of them. Something about seeing a big number on the scale didn't sit right with me. Even still, no matter how hard I tried, I just couldn't seem to lose weight. I wasn't obese by any standards and like I said, my curves could stop traffic, but my mother was from a different era. Getting dressed was always a struggle when I knew I was going to see my mother. If what I wear is too tight, she says something. If what I have on is too frumpy, she says something. I'm not sure why I always get so anxious since she's going to have something to say no matter what I wear, but I do. It never fails. I go through this whole "try it on-hate it-take it off" routine for a good hour or so before going back to one of the first few outfits I had on. This was yet another area of my life I should probably speak to a therapist about, but I stuff the thoughts and emotions down to the room in my heart I never enter.

I finally decided to throw on some jeans, a scoop neck top, and a long duster cardigan. I put on my favorite pair of wooden clogs and headed on out. The entire drive over there I was constantly speaking to myself. I told myself that I wouldn't let my mom get to me. I wouldn't answer questions about my love life, and I wouldn't let her body shame me. I would not walk out of there feeling so deflated that it would take weeks to pump me back up.

As I pulled up to my parents' house, I saw my brother's car in the driveway. Jacob was the poster child for the perfect son. He called every day, made sure they had everything they needed and never missed a Sunday brunch. He even tried to take them to all their doctor's appointments. Dad always resisted by says he was not at that season in his life where he needed "Driving Miss Daisy" accommodations. He said he has not hit anyone or anything, so he was still able to drive. After his cataract surgery, he didn't even need his glasses for driving anymore so he felt he was better than ever. I had to admit my dad looked good for his age and was in great shape. He could probably out walk me any day of the week and he still played tennis and golf whenever he could.

My mom, on the other hand, was perfectly okay with being chauffeured around. She never liked driving and always accepted Jacob's offers of driving her around because she said it allowed her to spend more time with him. Jacob was a straight up momma's boy which is probably why he couldn't keep a girlfriend. Most men have baggage like baby momma drama or the aftermath of a fatherless childhood, but Jacob's baggage goes by the name of Shirley Mae Patterson aka Momma Patterson. To Mom's benefit she made sure that her son was self-sufficient. Jacob was a great cook and meticulous when it came to keeping his home clean and maintaining a clean and polished look. He had his own thriving dental practice for 13 years with no signs of it closing any time soon. In short, he was Mom's pride and joy.

I have always been in his shadow. He was the overachiever of the family and I was considered the underachiever. My parents would never admit that, but they were always comparing us, and I could feel that my mom had a sense of disappointment with me. As her only daughter I think she expected so much more from me. If anything, at least the opportunity to plan my wedding with me and share in the birth of her grandchild by now. I have stopped searching for approval from her.

I would say that I was always more of a daddy's girl. He would do anything for me, and he was always there to help me out whenever I needed it. Mom said that he was too much of an enabler, but I just called it fatherly love. Regardless of my relationship with my mother, I always knew I was truly blessed to have grown up in a two-parent home with parents who instilled in us the value of working hard and being a person of integrity.

As I started to get out the car, I heard my brother scream from the front balcony, "Well, well, well look who finally decided to show up for a Sunday brunch. So nice of you to join us."

I rolled my eyes and said, "You know I love to keep you guessing and on your toes." I had other choice words for him running through my mind, but I wouldn't risk the chance of my parents hearing me say them.

He laughed and headed back in the house. He was probably going to run down and continue to harass me as I walked through the door. I took a deep breath and told myself I was ready for whatever lay ahead of me before proceeding up the front steps. As soon as my foot hit the landing, the door flew open and Jacob ran up to me and gave me the biggest hug. He whispered in my ear, "It's really great to see you."

I decided to tease him a little. "Yeah, now you don't have to have another boring brunch with just Mom and Dad. You know I have always been the life of the party!"

Suddenly, I heard my mom shriek and say," Elijah guess who's here, Morgan!" Even though I told her I was coming, my mom never expected me to follow through with what I said I was going to do because I have reneged so many times before. I couldn't tell from her tone whether she was really happy or just being sarcastic.

I walked in and saw my dad come from the kitchen with a big smile on his face. I stopped in my tracks for a second startled to see how old my dad looked. He had always been such a youthful looking guy that I never expected to see so many wrinkles on his face and both his head and beard fully gray. You could still see his muscular physique through his velour sweat suit, but I could definitely see that he was beginning to show his age. I gave him a hug and then walked over to hug mom. She stretched her arms out to stop me so that she could give me the Mamma Patterson once over and then she hugged me. Somehow, I think she believed that she needed to look everyone up and down first thing to get the real read on how they were (before they had time to start their acting out the façade they had already prepared prior to coming). Mamma Patterson had always been known as that sweet woman who pulled no punches and told it like it was. It's what we say, "She ain't got no cut cards." She didn't care whether you were Pastor So & So or President Whoever, you got no slack from her. She would always say right is right and wrong is wrong.

"Come on into the dining room Moosey. We were just about to sit down and say grace."

Since we were kids Jacob has always called me Moosey because I always walked around with this moose stuffed animal. I named it Moosey and one day Jacob said if I kept carrying that thing around, I would turn into Moosey. So since then he always called me Moosey. I didn't really mind until I got older and my friends began to tease me about it. I asked Jacob to stop calling me that because people were teasing me. He looked at me and said are you going to let people's actions change who you are and what traditions and customs we have set as a family. I didn't fully understand what he was saying, but I knew I had to respond no. If I said anything contrary, I would get a two-hour lecture from him about being my own person and not letting ignorant people dictate how I feel or change who I am. However, I did notice that after that he only called me Moosey when we were amongst family.

I walked into the dining room and saw that the table was set to perfection and the food was carefully laid out in the center. My mom had a wonderful way of plating the food so that it added to the décor of the table. Mom never used those aluminum tin pans or Tupperware to serve anything, not even when we had a barbeque. I could see Mom hastily adding a place setting to the table. I knew she was hoping I wouldn't notice that it looked more like an afterthought than a planned part of the table. That is how I sometimes feel being a part of my family, an afterthought. I always feel so out of place... like I don't fit in. Dad ushered me towards one of the previous set plates and sat at the chair in front of the last-minute place setting. That was just like my dad, always taking the bullet that was meant for me.

Once we all sat down my mom directed me to say grace. I knew that this was her way of seeing if I still had a relationship with God and she could surely tell by my prayer. I started to say, "Jay why don't you say grace" but decided against that. I was not going to fail the very first test she's given me. I wanted to walk out of there with a score of at least 50%. So, I pulled out one of the many stock prayers I heard from all the prayer breakfasts and revivals Mom made us go to. I first quickly asked God to bring one back to my remembrance and then pieced a prayer together. I said a strong amen not because of the Holy Spirit but because I was proud of myself for pulling one out the arsenal and passing with flying colors. Whew, one test down and probably thirty more to go.

We then began to pass the food around. It was so funny how even now we were still programmed on how we pass the food. We always wait for mom to pick up the first dish (she always started with the meat) and pass it to my dad. He was always first to serve himself and then he would pass it to my brother who would then pass it to mom and then to me. Each food item was always passed that way. I was always last to receive the food and sometimes there would only be as little as a teaspoon left.

I'll never forget one time when I was young, I got angry that I only got one piece of bacon and Jacob got four pieces. I fussed and expressed my dissatisfaction. My mom sternly replied, "Young lady you be grateful for what you have. Maybe God saw fit to allow you one piece only because He knows you need to fit into them clothes." I was so humiliated and embarrassed that I softly cried and never complained about the portions I was left with again. My dad saw my tears and slipped me two pieces of his bacon under the table.

After everyone served themselves my mom went into how great Jacob was doing and bragged about him doing a mobile dental clinic at the church for the youth next Saturday. I knew that all of that was just a dig at me in the hopes that I would get jealous enough to want to outdo him and as my mom would say, "Do something with my life." I chimed in that my boss might be transferring and that he was considering me for the GM position at the hotel. I thought that if my mom heard that I might be getting a promotion from Assistant General Manager to

General Manager she would lay off me a bit. Boy was I wrong.

"Ummm, it takes him leaving for you to be promoted. Your daddy didn't get to become president of G&M Construction by waiting for someone to leave. He walked in there already set to take over. He showed them he was better and earned that position."

Jacob could see my temperature start to rise and quickly chimed in, "That's great Morgan. I know he wouldn't give you that position if he felt you couldn't continue his great work."

Why couldn't our meals be like the Klumps in *The Nutty Professor*? At this point, I wouldn't care if it was Mom who morphed into four different people as long as we could experience the laughter that Eddie Murphy produced. What I wouldn't give to eat, laugh, and be merry right now as opposed to eat, be cut down, and get angry.

We pretty much ate the rest of our meal in silence. Every now and then Mom would try to initiate small talk, but no one was interested in talking. When the meal was over, I helped mom clear the table while Jacob started loading the dish washer. I told Mom to sit and relax with Dad in the living room while Jacob and I finished with the dishes. Once I was certain she was away from ear shot I flicked the dish towel at Jacob and whipped it back so fast that a loud pop came from his leg. We used to always flick each other with the towel to see who could create the largest red mark and leave the person screaming in pain. I was so good at it I would leave a mark on Jacob's leg that would last for days.

"So big brother, what's the TEA?"

He looked a little startled and stammered, "What do you mean?"

"I mean I know something is going on with you, so what is it?"

"Oh, so Mom told you?"

Mom told me? What was he talking about? Wow, if I play my cards right maybe he really will spill the TEA. "Uh, yeah. I wish I heard it from you. You know how Mom never gets the story right. So, you tell me yourself." I hope he couldn't tell that I had no clue what he was talking about.

"Morgan, I really screwed up. I was at a dental expo in Miami and met this girl who was staying in the same hotel as me. We got to talking and spent the rest of the weekend hanging out. She was a nice diversion from the dentists I usually hang with when I go to these things. We had a good time, but I never really thought any more of it after I left. Well she tracked me down a few weeks ago and told me she is five months pregnant. I am going to be a father."

I couldn't believe my prim and proper big brother was not only having a baby out of wedlock but by someone he really had no feelings for. How dare Mom walk around here acting like Jacob's stuck don't stick and rubbing it in my face knowing that her "Son" was about to have a baby with a weekend fling.

"Morgan, I don't even really know her. I don't know her background and what kind of mother she will be. Mom is insistent upon going to Miami and meeting her, but I'm not trying to let that happen. I mean you know how Mom can be. She would only make things worse."

"What does your baby mama want?" I asked him. He looked like I just kicked him in the stomach when he heard the words baby mama. Yeah Mr. Perfect you got a baby mama!

He went on to tell me that Marisol, his baby mama, doesn't want anything from him. She knew what she was getting into when they hooked up that weekend and wasn't expecting it to go any further. Besides, she was in a committed relationship and would rather he not get involved in things. She didn't want to mess things up with her boyfriend who was willing to help raise the baby.

"Who does this chick think she is saying she doesn't want you to have anything to do with the baby?" I yell out. I was angry. Not because I thought she was wrong, but at the fact that it was just like my brother to screw up yet still get out of it as if it never happened. You ever meet someone who always comes out of major screw ups squeaky clean. That was Jacob Denzel Patterson (yes his middle name really is Denzel). Karma always bypassed him. It made me sick. Why couldn't I have that luck?

"I just can't walk away knowing that my seed, my heir, my child is out there, and I am not a part of their life." He then turned away and started to wipe his eyes.

I was in total shock. I couldn't remember the last time I'd seen my brother cry. I thought for sure I would be the one with the royal mess up but nope; Jacob beat me to it.

"Well, you can only be absent from their life if you choose to be," I told him. I never thought I would be the one encouraging the encourager. Right when I was about to go into my Dr. Phil spiel my phone rung. I picked it up and heard Sebastian say, "Morgan, we have a situation at the hotel, and you need to get over here right away."

I gave a quick goodbye and headed over to the hotel. All kinds of thoughts were running through my head. What kind of situation? Could it be like the situation we had where a fight broke out with some bikers and thirty thousand dollars worth of property was destroyed? Or like the situation where some teenagers decided to put laxatives in the punch at their prom which resulted in poop all over our ballroom carpet and our pool towels having to be thrown out because they used them to wipe off the poop from their dresses and suits. Or was this situation similar to the time when a little girl found three guys getting busy in the laundry room. What the heck was I walking into?

As soon as I got to the hotel Sebastian ran out and told me to go with him to room 505. We were literally running up the stairs and I was huffing and puffing asking him what was wrong. When I entered the room, I was expecting to see a crazy scene, but I just saw Antonio and Ana standing next to the bed. I took a moment to catch my breath before asking them what was going on. They all looked at Ana who began to tell me exactly what was happening.

"Senora Morgan, I was cleaning the room when I found a bag under the bed. I pulled it out and it was open. I looked inside and saw money in it. I didn't know what to do so I called Antonio. He and Mario came to the room and I showed him what I found. We called down to Sebastian and he came up."

Everyone then looked at Sebastian, so I nudged his arm for him to continue.

"Well what had happened was…" Sebastian paused for a moment.

"Come on D we don't have all day," an exasperated Antonio blurted out.

"Ok, ok. When I got to the room Ana was acting like she was in a rap video and making it rain with money."

Ana immediately hit Sebastian and started yelling, "El mentiroso, liar, liar, liar!" She then threw Antonio under the bus. Antonio was the one who took the money out the bag and started counting it."

Antonio chimed in, "That was only after Sebastian started jumping up and down, throwing the bills on the bed and rolling around in them."

I threw Sebastian a "Oh no you didn't" look and he just put his head down. "Ok, ok just give me the bag please!"

"Well see, that is where we have a slight problem," said Sebastian. "We decided to count the money to see how much it was. So, we placed it on the bed, and we counted how much money was in the bag. Girl there was 60 grand in that piece! You hear me – 60 K, 60 thousand, 60 G's!!!"

"What! Where is it now?" I inquire.

"So, we got really scared that maybe this was drug money. We decided we better put it back in the bag. I figured we had to take it to your office, but I didn't want to be seen with the bag, in case the dealers came back. Ana suggested we go get the linen cart and hide it in there. I told Antonio and Mario to stay here and Ana and I went to get the cart."

Antonio interrupted to say, "Ms. Morgan, I specifically told Mario to watch the bag while I took a quick leak. When I came out the bathroom that fool was gone and so was the bag!"

"You're kidding me. Where is Mario now?" I was now beyond impatient and just wanted answers.

"We can't find him. We looked outside and his car is gone," said Ana.

"That idiot done ran off with some drug dealer's money. Now they all gonna come after us. They gonna chop off our fingers one by one until we tell them where the money is!!!" Sebastian clearly watched too many cop shows on tv.

Ana burst into tears and Antonio was dialing his crew ready to put an APB out on Mario.

"Sebastian, just shut up," I said while trying to figure out how I was going to tell my boss this one. "We have to call the police."

Ana began to lose it and Antonio started trying to console her while talking on the phone with somebody who I believe he called Slade. From the sound coming from the other end of his phone the cops better find Mario before Slade did.

"Antonio, I'm going to pretend I didn't hear what I just heard. I'm not going to be an accessory to conspiracy," I said as I narrowed my eyes at Antonio. I knew I wasn't exactly scary, but he knew I meant business.

"That damn fool!" Sebastian yelled briefly taking my attention away from Antonio. "I hope he knows I may look soft, but if it's either my ass or his, it'll be his mama slow singing.

Ana briefly stopped crying only to start chanting, "I'm not ready to die."

This time I put my head on my head. I felt a headache the size of Mount Rushmore coming on. These fools weren't even sure if it was drug money and they were already acting like bad actors from a soap opera. If drug dealers were going to come to the hotel, they'd have to kill all of them for sure because none of them knew how to keep their mouth shut.

Melissa Elizabeth

"All of you settle down," I said as I tried to gain control of the room. "You're all upset, but you have no idea where this money came from. It might not even be drug money.

"Oh, yeah your right. Chile it could be from a bank robbery. Didn't the bank off of Somerset Rd get robbed a few days ago?"

I wished I had a muzzle to put on Sebastian's mouth. Every time he opened it, something worse came out. I shot him one of my death stares and silently dared him to say another word.

"Why don't we all go downstairs to see who the last guest in this room was. Surely whoever the money belong to wouldn't have left it here on purpose."

Thankfully, no one objected. We all headed downstairs to my office. It was kind of hilarious how the three of them keep looking around fearful they were being watched. Ana was still upset when we got downstairs so I told her she could head home. She asked Antonio to walk her to her car. I told her I would call her later. I knew she would want an update and probably wouldn't be able to sleep if she didn't get one.

Ethel was working the front desk. She looked at us suspiciously and greeted us. I think she was hoping we would stop and tell her what was going on, but we kept it moving and went straight into my office. I heard her ask if we needed her help before I slammed the door shut and went right for the computer. We discovered that the room was issued to a Jeremy Collins. His billing address showed

99

he lived in North Carolina. Unfortunately, none of us could remember what he looked like, but we did have security footage we could retrieve from the cloud to give the police if it came to that.

"Umm, that don't sound like no drug dealer," Sebastian sighed.

"What exactly does a drug dealer's name sound like?"

"I don't know, but it doesn't sound like that."

"You can't tell whether or not a person is a criminal by their name," I scolded.

"That's a lie. Every Rontarius I ever met was a criminal. And Butch too. If you meet a man named Butch you may as well go ahead and get the money ready for his books because that fool is going back to jail within a month."

I tried to keep a straight face, but that Sebastian was such a nut I had no choice but to bust out laughing. It was the laugh I needed to release the tension. When I finally caught my breath, I gave him all of Mario's numbers and told him to keep calling and leaving messages to let him know we were calling the police.

Sebastian mumbled, "I am only doing this for you boss. As far as I'm concerned sticky fingers can get what's coming to him."

While Sebastian called Mario, I called the police. Within minutes they were at the hotel ready to speak with us. After hearing from all of us and getting our contact information they asked for all the information we had on Mario. The officers left their card with each of us and told us that if Mr. Collins contacted us in regard to the bag to give him the number of the police precinct and to be sure to state that the bag was turned into them.

Sebastian proclaimed loud and clear, "Oh you best believe Imma let 'em know it ain't here."

As the officers left out, I turned to Antonio who had mysteriously gone silent. He was hiding something, and I intended to find out what it was.

"Antonio, what aren't you telling us?"

"What are you talking about?"

"You're hiding something. I can see it on your face."

"You don't see anything on my face. I told you Mario was bad news but you just had to keep giving him chances. Now he's in the wind with a drug dealer's money."

"How are we back to the drug dealer theory?"

"Who said it was a theory?" Antonio asked mysteriously before he turned to leave my office.

I sat there with my mouth hanging open. Sebastian, on the other hand, seemed to be clueless. He turned to me and said, "Heifer you didn't bring me a plate?"

Before I could stop myself, I threw my stapler and yelled, "Get out!" Sebastian was lucky I was still trying to get back into his good graces or I would have made sure that stapler left him singing soprano.

Chapter Six:

Did I Just Hear a Dog?

As I walked into the hotel, I saw Ethel on the side of the front desk talking to some guy. She immediately turned red when she saw me.

"Hi Ethel," I said as my eyebrows questioned the scene I'd just walked in on.

"Hi Morgan. I didn't think you were coming in today."

"I didn't either. Markey Rain called out and I couldn't find anyone to cover her shift, so you're stuck with me.

"Um, I can't say I'm disappointed," Ethel said following me so she could get back to being behind the front desk where she should have been in the first place. The guy she was talking to made a quick bolt to the front door and left.

I thought that it was strange. "Ethel who was that guy you were talking to?"

"That was my son."

I thought it was weird she didn't introduce me to her son but assumed she was just a private person. "I didn't know you had a son.

"Yep, he lived in Atlanta for a while and just moved back home a few weeks ago. Him and his wife separated, and he is staying with me until he can find a job and a place to stay. I'm praying for reconciliation and healing though. You know God honors marriage."

I chuckled. "You just let God do it and don't go meddling in other folk's business."

The look she gave me let me know my unsolicited advice would fall on deaf ears. Ethel had a plan and waiting on God had nothing to do with it. I decided to let it go. Who was I to tell her she couldn't meddle in her son's life? My mother never stopped meddling in mine. I decided to change the subject.

"If Marley Rain calls out again, would you like to pick up some extra hours?"

"Of course, Sweetie. I am available any day but Sunday. You know Sunday is the Lord's day," Ethel responded.

How could I forget? That was the one thing she said was non-negotiable when I interviewed her. She said she would not and could not work on Sundays. She said in the 30 years since she gave her life to Christ, she missed only one Sunday service and that was the day her husband died. She told me the story of the morning of his death during her interview. It was a strange conversation for a job interview but after working in the hotel industry for so long, the story of a dead husband was far less shocking than many others I've heard. Even still, I remembered every word of the story.

Ethel woke up early one Sunday morning to pray before church. After her prayer time she prepared for church and then went to fix breakfast for her husband before leaving. After fixing breakfast she called up to him to let him know his breakfast was ready and she was headed out. Normally he responded by saying, "Okay baby, see you when you get home." But this time there was no response. She went upstairs to check on him and he was lying on the bathroom floor. When Ethel finished inappropriate story, she'd looked at me and said he had gone to be with the Lord. After hearing that, I didn't know what to say so I replied, "When can you start?" That was mt introduction to Ethel, and our conversations haven't swayed much since that day. I say something perfectly normal and mundane. Ethel finds a way to turn it into a hyper-religious conversation.

When I told Sebastian Ethel's interview story, he swore she used the sympathy card to get a job. He doesn't even think it's true. He believes she made it up. He thinks that Ms. Ethel is a freak and her husband died while they were having sex. I tell you that boy is a mess. I've always thought he would make a great screenwriter one day with the number of stories and scenarios he comes up with.

Sebastian called me a push over for weeks after that. He used to rub his eyes like he was crying every time he saw me. I used to tease him and say, "Yeah, I was such a push over that I hired your sorry ass." He quipped back that my life has changed for the better ever since. I always told him the jury was still out with that one.

Melissa Elizabeth

I snapped out of my revelry and noticed a woman walking around the lobby looking somewhat confused. I saw she had a suitcase with her, so I wondered if she has checked in yet.

"Ethel, do you recognize that woman over there?"

"No. If she's a guest, she checked in before my shift. This is my first time seeing her."

I realized I better keep my eye on her. I watched her for the next five minutes. She walked over to the refreshment bar and poured herself some water and took a few cookies. I noticed she took the oatmeal raisin and not the chocolate chip. Sebastian and I have a whole theory about people who chose oatmeal cookies over chocolate chip cookies. We think of them as those wannabe health fanatics who think that when it comes to eating the selection of the lesser of two evils puts you in the "health-conscious" category. They think that just because they take the stairs instead of the elevator, they are better than you. Who cares if they never set foot in a gym or never walked a mile? At least they are doing something. Those people really believe it's okay because they eat carrot cake as opposed to strawberry shortcake. They are okay smothering their salad with ranch dressing because it's the low-fat kind.

The wannabe health freak then sat by the fireplace and proceeded to make a phone call. She began talking softly but after about two minutes her voice level rose to football game level. I looked over at her and coughed loudly. This caused her to look up and mouth, I'm sorry. She then cuffed her hand around the mouthpiece of the phone and lowered her voice. Once she ended the call, you could see she was clearly agitated. I immediately put my guard up and decided that I should go over and check on her.

As I proceeded to walk in her direction the lobby door opened, and she looked over and waved at a gentleman. I slowed my trot and acted like I was checking on the refreshment bar. They hugged and proceeded to head to the front desk. I walked back to the desk and began to ear hustle as Ethel was checking them in.

The lady began to tell Ethel that her and her guest had met online and been dating for a few months. She said that many of her girlfriends had little to no success with online dating, but she was fortunate enough to strike gold on her first try. She told Ethel that they live five hours away, so they always meet each other halfway between the cities they each live in. Ethel told her that when her and her husband started dating, he was in the military and they had a long-distance relationship for three years. The woman grabbed the man's arm and looked up at him and said, "I hope ours doesn't last for three years."

I looked at them and smiled. The guy looked like he was not trying to have conversation and just wanted to get his key and leave. The woman talked to Ethel for about ten minutes after she gave them the keys. I was sure she would have talked longer if her boyfriend hadn't jerked her arm letting her know he was ready to go. She smiled at Ethel and thanked her for her assistance. Even though they walked off arm and arm she made sure to give him an earful. She obviously wasn't happy with his impatience. I heard him tell her, "But baby, I just don't want to waste any of our precious time together." She jumped in his arms, wrapped her legs around his waist, and gave him a big kiss. It was definitely one of those "Please get a room" moments. The jump caused him to drop his duffle bag. As I looked down at the duffle bag, I noticed something long hanging from the slightly opened part of the bag. It seemed as if the zipper of the bag was open. When he went to pick it up a dog collar fell out. I thought that long thing looked like a leash. The guy turned red and quickly picked it up. Our website, lobby doors, and front desk sign clearly states no animals allowed. If he was trying to sneak in a dog, he would be sorry when I charged his card a huge cleaning fee. I asked Ethel what room they were in. She told me 319. I made a mental note to remember the number.

Ms. Stein came up to the front desk a few moments later.

"Ethel, can you add these envelopes to the outgoing mail?"

"Sure Ms. Stein. How are you doing today?"

"I am doing really well Ethel."

"You certainly are Ms. Stein, for the good Lord woke you up this morning."

Ms. Stein smiled at Ethel and then turned to me and said, "Morgan, it's great to see you. How are you doing?" She asked as she walked down to the end of the counter where I was standing.

"I'm doing fine despite having to come in on my day off."

"You know Morgan, you are one hard working woman. You would make a great wife one day. The way you serve here at the hotel shows that you would serve your husband well."

I just looked at her thinking – he ought to be serving me. I guess the look on my face made her realize I was offended because she said, "Oh yeah, you modern day women don't believe in serving a man."

I just smiled and chuckled. I didn't feel like getting into an in-depth convo with her. I enjoyed talking to Ms. Stein more when she was talking about herself and not probing into my life.

Besides, is it so wrong to want your husband to cater to you and your needs? In this day and age where both the man and woman are working its only right that the tasks of the home are split. My husband is going to have to know how to cook, clean, and do laundry. Even if he gave me the option to stay at home, I think I am too independent of a woman to be dependent on a man financially. I want my own money and the ability to control how I spend it. I am not one to be asking for money from no man because I have none. If I am asking it's because I want to add to what I already have.

I remember there was a time that I didn't even have money to by feminine products and had to ask my dad. He took me through the ringer, making me explain what happened to my money and what I need the money for. It was devastatingly embarrassing to tell my dad I needed money for Midol and tampons. I vowed from that day forward I would never be dependent on someone for money.

Sensing I wasn't in the mood to converse, Ms. Stein stated that she was going to sit outside and have a smoke before her ride came to take her to her appointments. She shared that she had a full day of appointments and would not be back until later in the evening.

I headed to my office hoping that no one would bother me. I was going to get some online shopping done since I clearly couldn't get to the mall like I had planned. I was surely going to speak to Marley Rain about this one when she returned. That chick better be sick and not gallivanting around her parents' beach house in Ocean City.

What I wouldn't give to be at the beach right now. I always enjoyed being by the water. We have a sister hotel right on the beach where I can usually get a room during the off season. I went down there and worked for two months one time when the manager was on maternity leave. I got to know the staff well enough that if I was going to the beach for the day, they let me use their facilities without any hassle. I always staked a claim on the beach right by their hotel so I could run in and use their bathroom when I needed to. I hate the public bathrooms at the beach, and I am sorry, but the ocean is not a public bathroom as some may think.

After a while I heard a familiar voice out in foyer, so I got up and went to investigate. Sebastian was talking with

Ethel, and he was excited about something. He saw me and waved me over. He had the hotel megaphone in his hand.

"Hey Morgan. Girl come with me." He grabbed my arm and started running to the stairwell. I followed him up the stairs to the second floor and down the hall. I was starting to get tired and I was about to stop him and ask him what the heck he was doing but he stopped by the window and pointed down to a red corvette in the parking lot.

"Look!"

I rolled my eyes because I knew it must have been one of Sebastian's dumb schemes, but my curiosity got the best of me, and I looked down. I saw what looked like a naked butt in the air and the little car was surely rocking.

"Girl, I pulled up looking for a parking spot and noticed that car rocking. I couldn't imagine anyone would be in the parking lot having sex in broad daylight, but I saw a bare ass and knew someone was doing the do in the car. Here look!"

He shoved a pair of binoculars towards me. I was about to ask him what the hell he was doing walking around with binoculars, but he cut me off before I even started talking.

"Stop questioning every damn thing and look for yourself."

I looked through them and sure as heck I saw what looked like a woman straddling a man in the driver's seat. Sebastian then proceeded to pry the window open.

110

"Sebastian, what are you doing?"

He ignored me and yelled through the megaphone, "Well damn people get a room. For God's sake you are in front of a damn hotel!"

He must have startled them because the horn started blaring. It seemed as if in their effort to get up and cover up one of them got stuck in between the driver's seat and the steering wheel. Their knee was pressed up against the horn. For a good fifteen seconds the horn was going off which caused the few people in the parking lot to look. This embarrassed the frisky folks even more. The woman began to yell at the guy to drive off. After about two minutes they finally got the car in gear and pulled off, all the while trying to put their clothes back on.

Sebastian and I were cracking up. We laughed for a good ten minutes and then proceeded to head back down to the lobby.

"Sebastian what are you doing here anyway?" I asked him once I was able to stop laughing and actually speak.

"I was just leaving my boo's house when I got your message that you needed someone to work. I was only a few minutes away, so I decided to stop by and see if you still needed me."

I shake my head thinking Sebastian must be some sort of magnet for craziness because he seemed to always attract this kind of stuff. When we finally gathered ourselves and made it back to the lobby, we saw Mrs. Stein coming in

111

from outside. I cried out to her, "Hey Mrs. Stein, I thought you had left."

"I am trying to. This stupid ride share app says he is here, but no one has pulled up. I came to see if you could help me, Morgan."

I looked at her phone and sure enough it showed that a gold Camry had arrived to pick her up. I suggested we go outside and see. Sebastian, Mrs. Stein, and I walked outside looking for a gold car with the ride share logo on the side. We didn't see anything resembling that car. We then heard police cars and fire engines. Sebastian pointed over to the intersection right in front of the hotel and said, "Uh guys, I think we better order another pick up."

We looked over and saw a gold Camry had collided with the red Corvette we had just seen a few minutes ago. Sebastian and I looked at each other and both said at the same time, "I hope it was worth it!"

Sebastian said in true Sebastian form, "Um I betcha he didn't think that quickie ride would cost him his ride."

After helping Ms. Stein order another pick up on her phone app and waiting for it to arrive, Sebastian and I went back to my office. We ended up talking for a good two hours. I always enjoyed talking to him. Even though, most of our discussions involved him and his crazy antics or reminiscing about all the silly events that occurred at the hotel we did talk about some deep stuff. We have always been transparent with each other about the disappointment our mothers seem to have with us and our aspirations to prove to them that we were worthy of their love and respect.

I will never forget the time he cried like a baby telling me the story of how his mother kicked him out when she first found out he was gay. She called him a freak and said no son of hers would be caught sucking dick. He was homeless for three weeks before she would finally take him back. He said their relationship never fully recovered and there would always be a distance between them. That was why my mistake a few weeks back was so painful to him. I was the one person he was vulnerable with. Now that he'd forgiven me, I vowed to make sure I never hurt him again.

Ethel poked her head in and asked if I could step out for a minute. Sebastian stated that he better go and get some rest because he had to work tomorrow. We hugged and I told him I would see him tomorrow and he better not be late. I then went to the front to see what Ethel needed. Clive, our security guy, was standing at the desk talking with Ethel.

"Hey ya'll, what's up?"

"Several guests on the third floor have complained about a barking dog."

"I've walked the floor Ms. Morgan, but I didn't hear anything," Clive chimed in.

I immediately thought of the couple from earlier. "Remember the woman from earlier who checked in with the guy she met online?"

"Of course, how could I forget her. She probably would still be talking to me if her boyfriend hadn't stopped her."

"What room are they staying in?" I asked.

Ethel took a minute to search the computer and told me they were in room 319. I called Wynonna who was doing food service and asked her to prepare a seafood platter for me. The seafood platter was our code word for a fake room service order that we take to a room we want to check out because something fishy is going on.

I knew when I saw the dog collar and leash that those two were probably going to sneak a dog in. Guests tend to leave their pet in the car when checking in and then sneak them in later from one of our side doors.

Wynonna radioed me about fifteen minutes later and I asked her to meet me outside the third-floor elevator. Clive decided to go with me in case we had to ask the guests to leave. Sometimes guests get a little irate over being kicked out.

I got the tray from Wynonna and the three of us headed towards room 319. I grabbed Clive's arm signaling him to stop. We stood there listening. I figured this would look much better to my boss if we actually heard a dog barking and not just base it on the testimony of guests who can be known for pranking other guests by reporting false complaints to the front desk. Surprisingly, it only took about five minutes of waiting before we heard what sounded like a dog barking. Clive looked at me and said, "That sounds like it might be a German Shepard."

We approached the door and knocked. There was no answer, so we knocked again and said, "Room service."

After a few minutes, the same woman who talked Ethel's ear off opened the door and stated that they had not ordered room service. I proceeded to make up an apology while Clive tried to peek inside looking for a dog or evidence of a dog. He couldn't get much of a view because the woman was standing in the entryway with the door only slightly ajar. She then put the do not disturb sign on the handle and shut the door.

I asked Clive if he saw anything and he stated no. I told him to take the tray back and pick up the master key for me. I stood outside the room waiting to hear another dog sound. At first, I couldn't hear much but I did hear what sounded like a dog whimpering. I then heard several soft barks which then led into loud barking. I radioed Clive to hurry up and get back because there was definitely a dog in the room. When Clive finally got back, he was ready to bang on the door. I stopped him thinking the aggressive door knock may not be the way to go. I gave the door a gentle but firm tap. The woman answered a little quicker this time. Her lips were pressed firmly together, and her eyes looked like she wanted to kill me.

Without waiting for me to speak, she demanded to know what we wanted. Clive told her that there have been several complaints of a dog barking from this room and that we had to check to make sure she was not harboring a dog which was against hotel policy. The woman became even

115

more agitated and tried to block the door, but Clive was too far in and gently pushed her aside. I was right behind him as we looked for the dog.

To our surprise we saw the gentleman she checked in with naked on his hands and knees with a dog collar and leash wrapped around his neck. He immediately turned red and grabbed a sheet to cover his nether region.

I tried to keep my composure as I asked, "Where is the dog? We heard barking coming from this room."

"We don't have a dog," the embarrassed man proclaimed.

"You can stop lying. We heard the dog," Clive stated as he went to search the bathroom.

I proceeded to search the closet. I thought I had a pretty good idea of what was really going on but watching them squirm in shame was too much fun to stop.

The woman whispered, "Show them honey so they can leave us alone."

Her companion looked at her with pleading eyes. I knew he was begging her not to make him do it, but I was secretly praying she would. I had to see it myself. I silently wished Sebastian were there to enjoy this moment with me, but I knew if he were there, we'd both be fired for losing our composure in front of the guests.

"Just do it you idiot! Show them!"

The woman surprised Clive and I when her soft sweet tone was replaced by a scary sounding authoritative tone. We both just stood there staring at the man waiting to see if he would obey her commands. He was as read as a tomato, but that didn't stop him from howling and barking like a dog. My jaw dropped. This fool sounded just like a damn dog. Clive and I looked at each other in disbelief. I couldn't believe I was actually watching a naked man in a black sequined collar and long leash acting like a dog. The worse part was that he dropped the sheet, and I could see his impressive arousal growing with each bark.

I did my best to keep my eyes on their faces so I wouldn't become red with embarrassment. Clive and I started moving towards the door as I spoke. "Keep the noise down please. If I get any more guest complaints, I'll have to ask the two of you to leave."

They nodded their heads barely able to contain themselves. They looked like they wanted to resume having sex with Clive and I still in the room. Unwilling to let that happen, I started moving faster. In my haste, I tripped over a dog bowl full of dog food. I hurried to stand only to realize the woman had dropped her robe. She was completely nude holding a dog bone in one hand and a muzzle in the other. I didn't know when she had time to grab the items or when she took her robe off and I didn't want to know. It seemed our presence had only enhanced their freaky tryst and I was not about to spend one second longer than necessary in the room.

Clive and I raced out the room and headed quickly to the elevator. What kind of freaky mess was going on in there?

We waited until we were on the elevator before I acted like I was walking him with a leash as Clive barked and panted like a dog. The elevator pinged and we stopped before the door opened. A man and his daughter got on the elevator. The girl was wearing a backpack that looked like a dog and we just started cracking up. They looked at us like we were crazy. Clive told the girl he liked her backpack. She smiled and trotted off the elevator making dog noises when it arrived at the lobby.

We were about to tell Ethel what happened when she handed me a piece of paper with a number on it along with the name Detective Bradley on it. Ethel told me I got a call. I immediately forgot about the doggie couple and headed back to my office.

"Hey, I thought you were going to tell Ethel about the big fierce dog in room 319," Clive yelled.

"You tell her, I gotta make a call."

I dialed the number not knowing what to expect. I asked for Detective Bradley and my call was transferred. I discovered through the detective that they found Mario, our bag of money stealing dude, in Miami, Florida with a female who they believed also worked for the hotel. I asked them who and they told me her name was Marley Rain Harper. I was in shock. Sweet Marley Rain wasn't so sweet and innocent after all. Who would have thought those two would run off together?

The detective told me they were currently transporting them back to New Jersey and that he would be in touch. I sat in my chair for a minute in utter disbelief. Once I came out of my shock I yelled out to Ethel, "Hey Ethel, I think I am going to need you to work this weekend."

Chapter Seven:

Funeral Foolery

 I still can't get over the M&M crew," Sebastian said to me.

"What are you talking about now?" I asked. I could never keep up with all the "Sebastianisms" he came up with.

"You know, Marley and Mario. Who knew we had a regular Bonnie and Clyde up in this joint?"

"I know right!"

Never in a million years would I have imagined those two even talking let alone stealing money and running to Miami. They seemed like such opposites. But I guess what they say is true, opposites attract.

I once dated this guy my parents hated. He was what TLC would call a scrub. We were such opposites. I liked Anita Baker while he liked Public Enemy. We met in college at a time when I was looking to step out of the norm and explore new things. It was the perfect time because I was on a campus where no one knew the old Morgan from Brunswick High School. I could reinvent myself. I could change who I was and who I thought I wanted to be. So, this guy and I began dating. It wasn't anything serious just something to explore. We were complete and total opposite. Eventually those opposites weren't worth the aggravation. What was first exciting, turned into annoyance and frustration. Not to sound uppity or anything, but I felt as if he was bringing me down to a level I didn't want to be on. I decided that I should just stick to what I knew and what I wanted. I knew from that moment on, I'd never compromise or settle. That's probably why I was still single.

"Sebastian, I have something to tell you and you're not going to like it."

"Ah hell. Spit it out. What is it?"

"This weekend we have a funeral. The viewing is tonight, and the service is tomorrow."

"Morgan, I oughta slap the shit out of you right now. You know how I feel about being around the dead! Why would you put me on tonight?"

"I know, I know. I am so sorry. It's just with Marley Rain not working here anymore, I had no one else to come in. Maybe you can look at this as a chance to conquer your fear."

"Girl don't gimme that bullshit. You better hope I don't have a panic attack or pass out on you! I don't know why people wanna have a funeral at a hotel. Why can't they just have it at a church or a funeral home like regular people?

121

Who wants to be sleeping in a place where there's a dead body? It just doesn't make sense."

I could kind of understand where Sebastian was coming from. I mean I am all for breaking from tradition and the norm, but some things just aren't meant to be broken. To me, people have taken this concept of "not a funeral but a celebration of life" a little too far. I mean, what's the harm of actually mourning the loss of someone? It seemed as if now a days your sadness caused people to question your strength or as Ms. Ethel would put it, question your faith. It was like people equate sorrow to weakness or even mental and spiritual instability. It made no sense. I mean if I want to cry, I mean really cry, then I should be allowed to. This notion of having to be a strong black woman made me so angry sometimes.

I asked Sebastian if he ever had any regrets about not going to his grandmother's funeral. He looked up at me with such a look of pain and told me to basically "F-off" and he wasn't going there with me. It was quite obvious he was having a hard time with this. I knew this was going to be a long night.

I decided to leave him alone and hoped he wouldn't cuss anyone out during his shift. As I was about to head over to check on my buddy Winston who was working the bar, I noticed two guys grabbing a bunch of stuff out the store. I decided to detour and check to make sure these guys weren't trying to get the "five finger discount," as my dad would call it. I recognized them as the two young dudes who checked in with their mother. I wondered where she was. It was clear by the Versace bag and the well-manicured fingers holding up what looked like at least 20 carats in diamonds that this was a woman of means. I thought it strange that she and her two teenage boys would be staying at a hotel like this. They clearly seemed like Ritz Carlton people.

I pretended to check on the microwave located at the entrance of the store as they took their bundle and left out. I saw that they were walking towards the front desk and that they did in fact charge the items to their room. One of them mentioned how excited they were about graduation tonight and how they hoped to get a girl named Allie "lit" so that they could have some fun.

Just like that I knew their story. Quite often we got these rich white kids whose parents pay for a room at a hotel, so they have a place to "celebrate" after leaving the party sponsored by Mommy and Daddy. I've seen this done for birthdays and graduations all the time. Spoiled rich kids who think it's okay to party like a fool in a place that they don't frequent or wouldn't necessarily return to. That way, if they bust up the place or something bad happened it's no loss. Daddy cuts the check for damages and they go to another hotel next time. Those guys were pretty easy to finger out.

As Sebastian was charging their items, I saw a guy come up behind them. He was waiting to check in all the while staring at the boys like he recognized them. As the boys proceed to leave, he stopped them.

"Hey guys, has anyone ever told you that you have a face for the camera?"

I was thinking how many boys has he said that to? He needed to come up with a better pick up line. The boys pushed each other and started laughing. They told him no and then one boy told him his mom told him he resembled a young James Dean.

"I'm a film director. I'm staying here to work on my next film. Here's my card," he said as he reached into his pocket and retrieved a shiny black business card. "I'll be back in the office next week. Give me a call if you're interested in becoming a movie star."

The boys got excited and started down the hallway joking and calling each other names of various young actors.

I laughed and headed to check Winston out and see what he was up to. After about 20 minutes, my fun of chit chatting with him and drinking the delicious virgin peach daiquiri he made me was disrupted by my walkie talkie. I was being summoned to the front desk. I thanked Winston, took a few swigs of my drink, and headed out to the lobby. I glanced out the front door and saw a white van out front. Mr. Dupree, the owner of The Dupree Family Funeral Home, was talking to Sebastian.

We only worked with two funeral home as it relates to allowing them to use our facility to conduct services that require a group larger than 100 (their space could not accommodate functions more than 100). I appreciated the executives requiring them to be discreet when it came to transporting the body to the hotel. They were prohibited from using their standard vehicles of a hearse or van which has their name or logo on it.

Our hotel had a ballroom specifically designed with an entrance in the back of the building so funeral attendees did not have to go through the actual hotel. The architects also designed a separate entrance, which we called the service door. It was enclosed which made it the perfect way to discreetly bring the casket into the hotel without anyone noticing. It was an ingenious idea which added tremendous revenue to the hotel.

I could see Sebastian's anxiety level was already rising and we were just getting started. I immediately greeted Mr. Dupree and let him know Jacque would meet him at the service entrance if he would like to pull his car around to the back. Mr. Dupree said thank you and proceeded to head to the door then stopped and turned around and asked me how my dad was doing. Him and my dad were high school friends and rumor has it that Mr. Dupree had a secret crush on my mom, but my dad got to her first. I let him know that dad was doing great and that I would let him know he asked about him.

"Great, I am glad to see he is doing better!" Mr. Dupree smiled and went out the door.

Doing better? I didn't know what he meant by that. I was a little ashamed to admit that I hadn't gone over to see him or my mom since the Sunday brunch when I discovered my brother was going to be a father. I was counting the days in my head. Wow, was it really that long? Note to self, go check on my daddy ASAP.

I radioed for Jacque and Antonio to meet Mr. Dupree at the service entrance. I took a deep sigh and knew that I had to check on Sebastian. I knew this was something I would have to do periodically throughout the night. Another note to self, start looking for Marley Rain's replacement.

"Hey Sebastian, you okay?" I ask trying not to sound guilty even though I was feeling bad that he had to suffer because of me.

He rolled his eyes at me and began to do some meditation type breathing to calm himself down. It was hard to tell if he was serious about the breathing ritual or if he was just being overly dramatic. I figured it would be best to just let him go through and leave him alone.

I headed to my office and felt the urge to call my parents. I called the house. My parents were one of the few people I knew who still had the same landline from when I was a kid. The number has never changed.

After a few rings, I was mentally preparing the type of voice message I would leave when my mom's voice picked up on the voicemail. I was surprised when my actually answered the phone.

126

"Hi Morgan! It's great to hear from you. How are things?" Mom enthusiastically answers.

I told her things were great and that I was just calling to see how her and dad were doing. She told me that she was doing great and that Dad was ok. I didn't know how to take that comment about Dad, so I immediately wanted to speak with Dad, but don't want to offend her by asking for him too quickly. I knew I better give her time to talk with me, so I asked her what she had been up to. She told me all the things that were going on with her and after fifteen minutes I told her I was at work and couldn't talk long. I asked if I could speak with Dad and she paused for a second. After a few seconds of silence, she said that he was taking a nap, but she would be sure to tell him I called. I immediately looked at my computer screen and saw that it was 4 pm. It was strange that my dad was even taking a nap, but more so that the nap was at four in the afternoon. I looked at the schedule for next week and saw I was off Wednesday. I told mom I would call back Wednesday when I was off, and we'd have more time to talk. She said she would love that, and we said our goodbyes.

After what Mr. Dupree said and hearing the fact that my dad was taking afternoon naps, I decided I needed to go over there on my next day off. I told my mom I would call but I knew a popup visit would help me get to the bottom of what was really going on with Dad. I had a strange feeling that something was not right. My stomach started to hurt, and I couldn't tell if I was experiencing anxiety or hunger pains because I hadn't eaten all day. I called the kitchen and ordered buffalo wings and a salad. I asked them to make sure the wings were crispy and flats only. I headed over to the restaurant to eat before the Johnson family came for the viewing.

After eating I went to the Asbury Room where the viewing and funeral would be held. The room was modestly set up and Jacque was helping to organize the flower arrangements which had just arrived. As I was speaking to Jacque to ensure that everything was in place for when the family arrived, I couldn't help but look over at the "elephant in the room". It was a beautiful white and gold casket surrounded by a large array of floral arrangements in the colors of yellow and white. I kind of understood how Sebastian felt and immediately wrapped up by conversation with Jacque and went to check on the room reserved for the immediate family to gather. I saw Wynonna heading into that room and I followed her to ask her about the light refreshments that needed to be set up in the room. The round table was already set up with coffee and water and another table was being set up for the vegetable and cheese tray. Everything looked all set so I breathed a sigh of relief and went back up front to check in on Sebastian. As I was leaving the room, I saw a beautiful stoic black lady enter. She was a beautiful reminder of the great Dianne Carroll. She was being escorted by a very handsome young man. He looked at me and smiled but never took his full attention from the woman. He had eyes like Michael Ealy which caused my legs to weaken. I admonished myself for checking out a man who was obviously there to mourn the loss of a loved one. The man was fine, but I knew better. I turned my attention back to the woman he was escorting. They walked over to the casket and she placed her hand gently on top of it while closing her eyes as if to pray. Jacque came up beside me and informed me that they were the widow and her son. Knowing he was there to view his dead father's body made me feel even worse for checking him out. After about ten minutes, pretty eyes proceeded to escort her back to the door leading to the hallway.

Jacque whispered, "You should introduce yourself." He then slightly nudged me forward.

"Excuse me," I say as politely as possible. "Please accept my condolences for your loss. I'm Morgan, the Assistant General Manager. If there is anything you need this evening or tomorrow, please do not hesitate to ask."

"Mr. Handsome smiled and thanked me."

Dear God, the man had a set of perfectly straight white teeth that could light up the darkest room. And don't get me started on his skin. It looked like the smoothest butterscotch I'd ever seen.

When he extended his hand to shake mine, I nearly fainted from the jolt of electricity that coursed through my veins. It took everything in me for me to remain professional and I showed him and his mother to the private room prepared for them. Once we were inside the room, our eyes locked, and I became one hundred percent certain he was feeling me as much as I was feeling him.

This man was fine as hell. I normally wouldn't have grabbed a program, but I had to know more about this fine stranger. I saw the box located by the door and grabbed the program on my way out. I needed to get to my computer to start researching the mystery man as soon as possible.

When I got back to the front desk, Sebastian seemed to be in a better mood which made it much easier for me to tell him all about Mr. Fine Eyes. I told him about what happened, and we looked through the program together. I read the obituary of the deceased, Mr. Fredrick Johnson, to Sebastian.

As I was reading, I didn't notice that Mrs. Stein had come to the front desk and was listening in as I read. She then grabbed my arm and said, "What did you say? Please repeat what you said!"

"Fredrick Johnson is survived by his wife of 50 years, Carlotta Bennett Johnson; his son Randolph Johnson; his daughter Catherine Johnson; and a host of family and friends," I repeated.

She grabbed the program from my hand and read it for herself. Her face turned pale as if she had seen a ghost. She turned to the front of the program and read it. "So, the viewing is tonight, and the funeral is tomorrow at 10?" she asked.

"Yes."

"Where is it going to be held?" she demanded.

"In the Asbury Ballroom, located right past the pool."

Ms. Stein handed the program back to me and I could see her hands shaking more than usual. She abruptly turned away from me and slowly walked to the elevator without uttering another word.

Sebastian and I looked at each other. "I wonder what got into her," I say. Sebastian just shrugged his shoulders, snatched the program, and turned back to the obituary.

"So, his name is Randolph Johnson, uh?" He gave me a mischievous look and headed to the computer. Right when we were about to google his name someone said, "Excuse me."

We looked up and there he was – Mr. Fine Eyes himself. I immediately placed the program under a magazine and hoped he didn't hear a word we said. Sebastian gave him his hello that comes with several bats of his eyes as only Sebastian could do.

"I was wondering where I could get some hot tea for my mother," he asked; clearly directing his question towards me and not Sebastian.

I gently pushed Sebastian aside and said, "Don't worry, I'll take care of it. You go back to your mom and I'll make sure someone brings that to you immediately."

"Thank you," he said as we locked eyes again.

I quickly picked up the phone and called Wynona to arrange for hot tea to be delivered to the Belmar room where the family was gathered. I wanted to kick myself for not noticing that hot water and tea bags were not present with the coffee when I checked the room earlier.

"By the looks of things maybe you want to be the one delivering the tea," Sebastian said while giving me a look that made me feel like I had no idea how to catch a man. He then started feeling my shoulder. I pushed him away and asked him what the heck he was doing. He smirked and said, "I'm just checking to see how your shoulder is because you know cutie is gonna need one to cry on."

We started laughing and then noticed our two rich momma's boys were back. They were dressed in their graduation gowns and had two young ladies with them. They clearly looked a little tipsy and 4 of them were carrying duffle bags. They didn't even have enough sense to wrap the liquor bottles they were sneaking in because you could hear them clanging together in the bags.

Sebastian shook his head and shouted, "Congrats on getting a high…" He paused for a few seconds and they all looked shocked. "…school diploma." He finished before bursting into a loud fit of laughter.

The kids went from looking terrified to laughing along with him. Even though they were laughing, they seemed uncomfortable with us knowing what they were doing because they bolted for the elevator.

132

Surprisingly, the next few hours were rather quiet. I checked in on the viewing and it looked like the last of the family members were leaving. Mr. Fine Eyes was hugging a young lady telling her he wanted to get mom home to get some rest because the following day would be a long emotional one. I wondered if she was the girlfriend. I sized her up as we African American women do to each other. She was alright but seemed a little plain looking. He could do so much better. Besides, she had nothing on me.

When I got back to the front, I saw the maintenance guy Antonio. I told him to make sure that all doors of the Ashbury Room are locked and secured. We didn't want anyone getting in.

Before I could finish my sentence, Sebastian added, "Or Mr. Johnson getting out."

We all started laughing but as I look at Sebastian, I knew he wasn't joking.

Right before midnight, as I was preparing to leave, I decided to check the Asbury room to ensure the doors were locked. I had a think about making sure I double checked important things before I left work. If I didn't, I'd end up dreaming about work all night. I looked over at Sebastian and saw he was gathering his things as well.

"Sebastian, will you come with me to the Asbury room? I need to double check to make sure Antonio locked the doors"

"Are you out of your mind? Hell naw!"

"Please Sebastian. It's not like I am going in. I am just checking the doors."

After several pleas Sebastian reluctantly agreed to go with me. As we were heading down the hall towards the Asbury Room, I could see Sebastian getting more and more nervous. His breathing was becoming heavier and a fresh coat of sweat was gathering on his forehead. I couldn't believe he had such an issue with dead bodies. As we got closer, we heard a sound coming from the Asbury Room. Sebastian immediately stopped and grabbed my arm.

"I told you I ain't want to do this!" Sebastian yelled loud enough to wake the dead.

I put my finger to my mouth to get him to be quiet so I could determine what the sound might be. I was trying to put on a brave face, but I was getting a little scared myself. Suddenly we heard a loud crash coming from the room.

"Shit! This is why black people always die first in horror movies! Bye Morgan!"

Before I could respond, Sebastian was a fury of color running away from me. I didn't have time to worry about him. I ran to the door closest to me and it's locked. I rushed to the second door and it was locked as well. I was panicking but I knew the sounds were coming from inside of the room so the third and final door had to be unlocked. I tried the knob without realizing how hard I was pulling, and the door flew open almost making me lose my balance. As soon as I opened the door, I spotted the four graduates gathered around Mr. Johnson's casket which was on its side on the floor. Poor Mr. Johnson was hanging out of the casket. The girls started screaming as soon as they saw the dead body.

"What the hell is going on here," I screamed. "Somebody better get to explaining real quick!"

Both boys were giggling and you could tell they were drunk.

"We're sorry! We were just trying to find the pool, but it was locked, so Chad convinced us all to look around. He said a film director was staying at the hotel and that this room was probably set up for the movie filming. Brad thought it would be cool to get some pictures of the casket so we could post them on our Snap. He tried to jump on it and the casket fell over."

The words tumbled out of her like word vomit. Her face was pale, but it was clear she would make a great lawyer in the future if she wanted to go that route. While the boys were just starting to get the seriousness of the situation, she had already spoken up for the whole group.

"We're really sorry. We didn't realize it was a real body," Brad said a little too late.

I was furious and wanted to give them the third degree, but I knew getting Mr. Johnson back in his casket and it back up on the platform was more important. I yelled for the two boys to help me move the casket up right so we could get Mr. Johnson back in it. Both boys looked at me like I was crazy.

"Unless you want me to call the police and have them charge the 3 of you with tampering with a dead body, I suggest you get over here and help me right now."

I wasn't sure if that was a real crime or not, but I needed the bluff to work. I couldn't take the risk of anyone else coming into the room and seeing Mr. Johnson outside of his casket.

My bluff worked. Chad and Brad quickly lifted the casket while I gently placed my hands behind Mr. Johnson's shoulders. I tried to lift his upper body back into the casket, but he was so heavy that I couldn't do it by myself.

"Girls come help me," I yelled.

One of the girls was so hysterical she was no help but the other one pushed the front of the body while I lifted from the back and we were able to get him in. His hair piece had fallen on the floor and the linens that were in the casket were all over the place. I shut the top of the coffin and realized I better call Mr. Dupree and let him know what happened. Chad and Brad were apologizing to me profusely while the one girl finally got weeping Wendy under control.

Brad began to hit Chad telling him he knew this was a dumb idea. Once the girls had regained their composure, they really let the boys have it. They screamed that they were leaving and never wanted to talk to them again. They left cussing and fussing while the boys followed behind trying to get them to stay.

Melissa Elizabeth

I couldn't believe Antonio. I told him to make sure all the doors were locked. I looked at me phone and saw it was almost 1 am. I knew I better lock that door and get back to my office and call Mr. Dupree. He would need to send someone over first thing in the morning to fix Mr. Johnson and his messy casket.

After speaking with Mr. Dupree, I headed out to the front desk to say my goodbyes to the front desk attendant on duty. As soon as I walked out, I saw Brad and Chad checking out. They looked at me and opened their mouths to speak.

I threw my hand up to stop them. "Just leave."

I asked the attendant if he'd seen Sebastian. He said that the last time he saw him was about forty minutes ago when he ran through the lobby and out the door.

I managed to get a few hours of sleep before dragging myself back into the hotel early the next morning. I got up earlier than I wanted because I knew I had to make sure that the Mr. Johnson fiasco got fixed and I needed an extra thirty minutes of prep time in case I ran into Mr. Fine Eyes.

I didn't even go to the desk when I arrived. I headed right to the Asbury Room. I was so relieved to see the Dupree staff working to fix the body and the coffin. I turned to make a beeline to the door so they wouldn't stop me and slammed right into Mr. Fine Eyes.

I turned five shades of red and apologized. This man smelled like heaven. Despite my embarrassment from

137

running into him, I wished I could have laid my head on his chest and basked in his delicious scent. He gently placed his hand on the lower spine of my back and asked if I was okay. Oh Lawd... help me. That was my sweet spot.

"Excuse me. I didn't mean to startle you. I was just coming to check to make sure everything was okay before the service."

I didn't realize I was still standing so close to him until I felt the vibrations from the base in his voice course up and down my body. I knew it was a sin for a man to be this fine, but he was one sin I was willing to commit. I took a small step back and tried to compose myself.

"The funeral home is checking on the casket. You should probably wait a few minutes before entering."

"Thank you for the heads up," he replied before going to sit on the nearby chaise.

I knew I should have just walked away but I felt drawn to him like metal to a magnet.

"Is there anything I can do for you? I asked as I walked over to him.

Before he could respond, he rose to greet that chick from the day before. I was now in my feelings but snapped out of it and quietly slipped away.

On my way back to the front desk, I noticed Mrs. Stein outside the Belmar Room speaking with Mrs. Johnson. They hugged each other, and Mrs. Johnson quickly dipped back into the room. Mrs. Stein turned to leave. Her jaw dropped when she saw me.

"Mrs. Stein, I am surprised to see you here. I didn't know you knew Mr. Johnson. Are you staying for the service?"

"Oh, no dear. I know what it is like to lose a husband and wanted to give my condolences to his widow. From one widower to another. I can empathize with what she is going through."

We walked back to the lobby without saying a word. Mrs. Stein always seemed like she was okay, but I couldn't imagine what she was feeling at that moment. It didn't occur to me that the funeral would cause her to rehash her own loss and pain. She stated she was going upstairs to rest.

"Would you like me to walk you to your room?

"No Dear. I'll be fine."

We exchanged our usual hug and she said she would stop by before she went to the restaurant for dinner.

I went to my office to check out some resumes. Hopefully, I could schedule some interviews next week and have a new hire within the next few weeks. When I got to my computer I saw my screen was on Google. I forgot that before I left, I was going to google Mr. Randolph Johnson but after what I witnessed this morning I decided to not even bother.

A few hours later, I heard a soft knock at my door and saw Ethel at my door with a big grin on her face. "Morgan there is a nice gentleman at the desk asking for me."

"I'll be right there," I replied as I continued working. I wanted to immediately jump up but didn't want Ethel to think I was "thirsty" so I just played it cool. I waited about two minutes and then walked out front. I saw it was Randolph, and I smiled inside.

"Mr. Johnson, I hope everything went well with your father's homegoing and you're pleased with our service. It was our goal to make this difficult time a little easier for you and your family."

He smiled and proceeded to respond but was distracted by that pesky chick again.

"Mother is ready to go," she said.

"Okay," he said to her before turning his attention back to me. "My sister and I would like to thank you for all your help. It's never easy with the passing of a parent, but you and your staff helped us to focus on honoring his legacy."

Did I hear him say sister? I felt my heart leap inside of my chest.

"No need to thank us. That's what we are here for."

He turned to walk off but then turned back around and told me that he has his own business and to contact him if he could ever return the favor. He handed me his card. I took the card and casually put it in my pocket. Maybe I

140

would google him after all. It wasn't like men that fine walked into my life every day.

Chapter Eight:

Don't Take It for Granted

On Wednesday morning I headed over to my parents' house. Things hadn't been sitting well with me after my talk with Mom. I was concerned about my dad and I want to see what was going on with my own eyes. I wanted to call my brother to see if he knew anything but with his baby mama drama, I didn't want to bother him. I still chuckled when I thought that my "perfect" brother wasn't perfect after all. I decided I should check in on him later just to see where his head was at. Last time we talked it was all new and you could tell he was scared.

As I drove through my old neighborhood, I saw nothing had really changed on the surface. The houses all looked the same, but you could tell the people living in them were different. By the looks of the lawn ornaments and porch flags I could see that no area was immune to gentrification. As I pulled up to my parents' house, I saw our neighbor, Ms. Ellie, watering her plants on her front porch. She was one of the last few remaining original neighborhood folks. Back in the day, we didn't need a neighborhood watch with

Melissa Elizabeth

Ms. Ellie around. She knew all that was going on within our little block. If she wasn't sitting on her porch being nosey, she had her recliner positioned in her living room where all she had to do was pull open the corner of her curtain to see what was happening. She knew everyone's routine and everyone's car so if a suspicious car was driving down the block, she was on it. I could never sneak in and out the house without her knowing it. I could never understand how Ms. Ellie could inform Mom so quickly about what time I broke curfew the night before. To this day, I haven't figured that one out.

As soon as I got out the car, Ms. Ellie was calling my name. I walked over to her and asked how she was doing.

She replied, "Oh I'm fair to middlin." Ms. Ellie grew up in the south but never lost her southern dialect. "But I never see you around anymore. Your parents are getting older. They need you. I see Jacob all the time, but you're the daughter. You should be helping take care of them."

Ms. Ellie wasted no time. She jumped right into a rant that really wasn't any of her business, but I was raised to respect my elders, so I kept my opinion to myself. "I've been really busy with work," I said before quickly changing the subject by telling her how great she looked. My diversion worked. She lapped up the compliment and I quickly said goodbye before she could launch into another verbal assault.

I sprinted to the house. When I walked in, I screamed for Mom and Dad. Mom came out the kitchen fussing, "Shhh Morgan, your gonna wake up your father."

"Wake him up? What is he doing sleep at 11 am? Daddy used to be the first one up in this house," I responded.

"Well things have changed and we're getting older now. Ain't as easy to get up as it used to be," she said giving me a hug. I was surprised because Mom was not the affectionate type. "What are you doing here?" she inquired.

I told her I wanted to surprise her and Dad with a visit. I handed her some glazed doughnuts from her favorite bakery. She told me to come in the kitchen and she'd make some coffee.

When I walked into the kitchen it was like a time warp. Mom hadn't changed a single thing since I was a kid. She still had the same seventies décor including the wooden fork and spoon that all families had hanging on their kitchen wall. Jacob and I used to joke that we would one day take them down and actually try to eat with them. I think if we took them down, you would probably still see their outline because of the old, faded flower wallpaper plastered on all the walls. Obviously, accent walls weren't heard of back then.

Mom told me to get two mugs from the cabinet. I opened the cabinet and searched for two mugs with matching saucers. Mom was a stickler for that. Don't bring her no coffee cup without a saucer. I noticed as I grabbed the cups that she still had the ugly mug I made for her in camp one year. Every year mom made us go to this day camp at our local park. Jacob and I definitely had plenty of stories to tell about our camp escapades.

Melissa Elizabeth

Camp was where I had my first kiss. It was with Bobby Foster. I ended up smacking the mess out of him because a kiss wasn't enough for him; he tried to put his hand up my shirt. He was so pissed that I slapped him that once the shock wore off, he cussed me out and called me every name under the sun. After that he, stopped talking to me and began hanging around Noreen Cole.

Noreen Cole was not the most attractive girl but was known for being fast. The guys used to run their hand through her kitchen, which is what we called the back part of a black woman's hair right at the top of her neck. They then would pull it back quickly acting like they got cut. When a boy did that it meant that your hair was so nappy it could cut someone. Though they teased her about her hair, they all enjoyed feeling on her booty and any other body part she let them touch. I could never understand why she let them tease her about her hair in public but touch her everywhere else in private. Now that I was older, I understood low self-esteem made young girls and grown women do some really crazy things for male attention.

"Mom, I can't believe you still have this ugly mug I made you."

"Yup. I even have all of your and Mother's Day cards and homemade Christmas ornaments."

I shook my head and handed mom the mugs. She filled them with coffee and sat down at the table. I opened the box of doughnuts and we dug in. Dad came in the kitchen.

145

"Hey baby girl, I didn't know you were coming today," he said with a bright smile.

I got up to give him a hug. When I hugged him, I could feel how thin he had gotten. I kissed him on his cheek and noticed how his once puffy cheek had lost its puff. "How are you feeling, Dad?"

"Oh, I'm hanging in there for an old man," he said while slowly sitting down in the chair. "Looks like someone brought our favorite." He continued as he grabbed two glazed doughnuts. "So, what's shaking baby girl?"

Mom left to table to make a cup of tea for Dad as I told him all about the incident with Mario and Marley Rain. I told him about the psychic convention incident and the people having sex in their car and then getting into an accident when they sped away. Dad listened like my stories were the most interesting things he'd ever heard. This was another thing I loved about him. He was a great listener. I'd purposely saved the true reason for my visit until the end. I needed to loosen him up before I mentioned Mr. Dupree.

"I saw Mr. Dupree the other day. He asked me how you were feeling. It was almost as if he thought you were sick or something."

I noticed mom look over at dad. Dad chuckled and said, "Dupree must have gotten me mixed up with someone else. He might be starting to get the Timers."

146

Melissa Elizabeth

Timers was my Dad's way of hinting at Alzheimer's. I made sure to look closely at mom, while we were talking. She turned her attention from Dad and looked at her coffee mug like some foreign object was in it. What the heck was going on?

I let it go and we spent the next two hours reminiscing about old family memories. It was really nice to spend some time with my parents. Surprisingly, Mom was rather nice to me. Maybe Dad wasn't the only one changing.

"Are you staying for dinner? Mom asked.

"No. I have a few errands to run."

Mom grabbed my hand, yet another untypical action for her. "Your father and I would love to have you stay."

She was looking me straight in my eye with a sense of urgency I'd never seen from her. "I'll stay," I said.

Mom breathed sigh of relief as she looked at the clock on the stove. "Come on. My shows are about to come on."

We all went to the tv room. Dad sat in his recliner. Like many households, my parents had a recliner that was reserved specifically for the man of the house. It had a snack tray next to it to put remotes and Dad's libation of choice. Mom and I sat on the couch and we all settled down to watch the lineup of shows which had become a daily ritual for them.

"Morgan honey, wake up." My mom was shaking me to get up.

"Oh, sorry Mom. I must have fallen asleep somewhere between the judge show and the celebrity talk show you always watch."

"Come, help me fix dinner."

I took a few minutes to get myself together. I was having some good sleep. As I sat on the couch and looked around so many memories flooded back into my mind. Like the time Jimmy and I were sitting on this very couch watching the Jackson Five show. He was my first crush. His mom would work late so after school he would come over and hang out until his mom got home. I would never forget the time we were watching an episode and we began to pretend to be little Michael Jackson. We tried to out dance and out sing one another. We laughed so hard that I almost peed myself. What I wouldn't give to go back to those days when the only care you had was praying for a foot of snow so you wouldn't have to go to school. Life back then was about playing jacks and jumping rope with your friends.

I got up and moved closer to the mantle where Mom had all kinds of pictures lined up of us when we were kids. She seemed to have a lot more of Jacob than me, but I attribute that to him being the first born. I heard Mom humming in the kitchen and realized that I had momentarily forgotten that I was supposed to be in there helping her get dinner ready. I turned to head into the kitchen and saw my dad sleeping peacefully in his recliner. He looked like the way I felt as a kid, not a care in the world. I leaned over, gently kissed his cheek, and whispered in his ear, "Love you Dad." He smiled in his sleep.

When I got to the kitchen, Mom already had the pots going and was putting something in the oven. "What's that Mom?"

"It's the roast I made yesterday. I'm just warming it up."

I never understood why Mom hated microwaves so much. It was obvious we were having leftovers for dinner. If it were me, we would be making plates and heating them up in the microwave. Mom on the other hand, rarely reheated food in the microwave. She always complained that the food would get cold too fast and liked using the good old fashion stove and oven for reheating. I couldn't live without my microwave. I nuke everything from hot water to eggs.

Mom asked me to set the table for dinner. I began to gather the plates and utensils when I stopped and turned to face her. "Mom can I ask you something?"

"Sure, what is it?"

"What is going on with Dad?"

Mom stopped stirring the pot, put the spoon down, wiped her hands, and sat down at the kitchen table. She began to tell me that last year they noticed Dad losing energy as well as his appetite. They went to the doctor and discovered that his prostate had to be removed. He got through the surgery and they thought he would be fine. However, his symptoms of low energy and not wanting to eat remained.

They'd done all kinds of tests but still didn't know what was going on with him.

"We have an appointment in three weeks to see a specialist in New York. Hopefully, they can tell us what is going on."

"Mom, why didn't you tell me?"

"Your dad wanted to wait until we knew something definite. He didn't want to worry you about the surgery or how he was feeling."

I became a little upset but knew I needed to maintain my composure. My family acts like I can't handle bad things after what happened when my grandmother died. I kind of went into a depressive state that took a few months to get out of. My dad was so worried he would sometimes sleep over on my couch because he was afraid of what I might do to myself. I eventually went to see a therapist. I spent two years in treatment. She helped me through a lot of things and helped me discover that my grandmother's death was just a trigger for more deep-rooted issues I was having.

"Mom, I know I scared everyone when Grandma died, but I am much stronger now. I really wish you all would stop treating me like I can't handle things. I want to be there for you, Dad, and Jacob. Please don't rob me of that opportunity."

Mom smiled at me like she was seeing me for the first time. "I promise to work on keeping you informed, but out of respect for your dad's wishes, can you keep this conversation between us? It'll be best to wait until he tells you himself."

"Yes ma'am. I can do that."

Mom stood and hugged me. As soon as you finish setting the table, we can eat. The food should be warm now."

As I finished setting the table, I couldn't help but think about my dad. I even said a little quick prayer to God asking him to cover and protect him. Ms. Ethel must be rubbing off on me. My head was swarming with all kinds of possibilities of what might be wrong from cancer to a possible vitamin deficiency. If this was what my head was taking me through, I couldn't imagine what him and Mom might be thinking. I then asked for God to reveal to the doctors what was going on and to do it soon.

I ended up staying until late into the night. We had a great dinner. Afterwards, I played Dad in a game of 500. I remembered how we used to play that game all the time. I loved playing card games and I owed my dad for that. He taught me many of the card games I still played, Spades, Pitty Pat, Gin Rummy, and Crazy Eights.

After we played a few rounds, I told him that I better get going. I had several interviews for Front Desk people the following day, and I wanted to be well rested.

"I really appreciate you coming over baby girl. I hope you'll come over more often."

"I promise I will." I said as before I kissed them both on the cheek and said goodbye.

Hotel Chronicles

As I drove home, I began reflecting on my day. I never would have imagined that I could spend the entire day with my parents and actually enjoy every minute of it. So much so, that I couldn't wait until the next time I could visit. Wow, I began to actually get a little emotional.

The next day I couldn't wait to get into work. I had three interviews and I was really hoping one of them could be Marley Rain's replacement. I had a call out that morning so my day would begin with me covering the front desk for two hours until Ms. Ethel arrived. I kind of enjoy working the front because you get to really interact with the guests and hear some very interesting things.

Just the other night a guy came down saying he was waiting for his friend. While he was waiting, he proceeded to tell Ethel and I that for the past few days he had been having pain when he urinated. He then said that he'd just used the bathroom and blood came out. He had the nerve to ask us if we thought he should call his doctor. Ethel and I looked at each other like "duh" and I replied, "Uh, hell yeah." He told us that we were probably right, and he would call the next day because right know he had a visitor. He then waved his hand to a young gentleman who walked up and gave him a big hug. They walk off arm and arm. It took every ounce of me not to scream to his friend, you know he's peeing blood don't you!

I never understood why people feel so open to tell all their business. Whether it's to a complete stranger or posting it on social media, some things are better left between you,

152

your closest friend, and God if you asked me. You would never catch me spilling my stuff on social media or to a stranger. Google is alive and well and I sure as heck would never tell strangers my business. However, I knew some folks just wanted a listening ear. For some reason, they felt comfortable enough to open up to me and just share what they were going through.

As I was working the front desk, a woman came in to request a room. As I gathered her information, I saw she was from out of town.

"Are you here on vacation?"

"No, I'm here to be with my son,"

"So, your son lives here?" Maybe all the small talk we make at the front desk is what makes guests want to tell us all their business. Yet, if we said nothing while we checked the guests in, the awkward silence would make us seem rude.

"Uh no, he is a patient at Children's Hospital. He has terminal cancer and is about to enter hospice care. I have been staying at the hospital's long-time residence center for families here in town, but I just can't stay there anymore. I can't be around families who have sick or dying children. I hate to walk in there and see families with the same look I probably have. That look of trying to keep it together, but their eyes show their pain. Last night while in my room I heard a woman crying. I think it was coming from the room next to mine. I just needed to get out of that environment. I had to get away. Some would call me a bad mother for not being at my child's bedside right now, but

I don't care. I can't take anymore right now. I want to go to your restaurant and have a meal and a few drinks, sit by the pool, and maybe even get in the jacuzzi."

She stopped talking and just looked at me. I immediately understood what she meant. Her eyes were filled with sadness. And although she just spewed her business all over the check in counter, I understood her need to do so. She looked as though she would have exploded if she hadn't said the words aloud.

I couldn't even imagine what she was going through. Watching your child get sick, hoping that doctors could fix him, and then having to watch as they start to transition from this earthly place to their heavenly resting place. I could only image the depth of a pain a parent would feel watching all of that unfold.

As she took her room key, she said to me, "You know, you asked me if I'm here on vacation and I said no. I take that back. Yes, I am on a vacation. I am vacationing from seeing my child dying. I am vacationing from the pain of being helpless. I am vacationing from having to look like I got it all together. I am vacationing from the looming shadow of death that never leaves my side."

"I hope you enjoy your vacation and that it provides you everything you need," I said before she walked away.

After hearing her story, I couldn't help but think of my dad. I hoped I'd never have to take such a vacation, that whatever was going on with my dad didn't result in a long process toward an inevitable end. What if that specialist told us he was terminal? I mean you always know that each one of us will one day die but was I ready for my daddy to? My head was spinning, and I start to feel like I was going to be sick. This was all too much for me right now. I walked through the archway that led to the back office. I stood against its wall hiding. I started to cry, and I couldn't stop. I began to say to myself God, don't let him die, don't let him die. After a few minutes of tears, I gathered myself together and headed back up to the front desk. I guess this was what that lady meant when she said she had to hold it all together.

Chapter Nine:

It Goes Down at the Bar

The bar was unusually packed, for a Wednesday afternoon, but the staff seemed to be handling the orders efficiently. I walked in and took a seat next to our regulars George and Lauren. The couple stopped by the hotel every Wednesday to attend the auto auction. We'd grown accustomed to them and their antics. Today looked as if it would be no different.

"Hey Morgan," George said when he noticed me. "I got something for you."

I smiled knowingly. "You always have something for me."

George got off of his stool and moved to the one on my right, effectively sandwiching me between him and his wife. He smiled as he handed me a small bag. I peeked inside to examine my latest gift. A large smile spread across my face. I knew my hint about wanting to try pineapple martinis would work. George and Lauren always brought me small bottles of liquor. Not the cheap stuff, I'm talking the smoothest liquor I've ever tasted. Last week I'd mentioned wanting to make pineapple martinis so I could pretend I was on a tropical island. They'd taken the bait and rewarded my kindness with bottles of coconut rum and pineapple rum.

"You two are always so good to me. Thanks for this! I'm going to enjoy cracking these babies open this weekend."

"Why wait for the weekend?" George questioned as the wind from his w's hit my nostrils. I could smell the evidence of his refusal to wait. George's breath smelled at least 180 proof. I don't think I'd ever seen the man sober. They'd been coming to the hotel around 11am every Wednesday for years and the man was always drunk when he arrived. Lauren spent her time helping him remain upright in between her smoke breaks.

"We know you never wait, George," Lauren chimed in giving me a whiff of her stale cigarette breath.

The combination of their breath was more than any one woman could handle. I decided to try to order some food hoping that if they started eating, they'd stop talking. I motioned for Angela, one of the bartenders to come over.

"Hey Lauren, Morgan, and George! What will it be this week?"

The three of us placed our usual orders and Angela walked away to enter them into the computer. Out of the corner of my left eye I saw a dorky looking guy talking to a woman who looked far too attractive to be interested in him. My first instinct was to make sure she wasn't a prostitute. We've had our fair share of high-priced prostitutes try to work our bar. I asked Lauren if we could switch so I could monitor the two. Loving drama and gossip as much as Sebastian, Lauren agreed.

After we switched seats, I pretended to watch the television hanging from the ceiling as I spied on the couple's conversation.

"Do you live in this area or are you visiting?" the dorky guy asked the woman.

"I'm visiting. Why would I be at a hotel if I lived in the area?

The dorky guy realized the perceived silliness of his question. I knew his question wasn't silly though. Many locals frequented hotels. I was sitting right next to a couple who visited the hotel every week. He stuttered trying to come up with an answer. The woman must have sensed his uneasiness because she spoke up to rescue him.

"I'm here on business and decided to have lunch here instead of fighting traffic to go to another restaurant."

"So, you're staying here?"

This time I couldn't stop myself from rolling my eyes. The woman was obviously out of his league and feeding him great conversational lines and the dork was still messing it up. I was surprised she didn't cut her losses and move on, but she seemed to be interested in him. I couldn't understand why, but she seemed to really want to keep talking to him.

"Yes. I'm staying here at the hotel. I'm on the fourth floor. What about you?"

"Me?" the dorky guy almost spit out the soda he was drinking.

"Yes," she said with an obviously flirtatious laugh. Are you staying at the hotel?"

"Yes. I'm on the fourth floor too."

"What a coincidence. Maybe we'll run into each other tonight. Would you like that?"

Man, this woman was laying it on thick. She was sounding more and more like a working girl to me. There was no way a woman who looked like her wanted to be with the dork who couldn't hold an intelligent conversation if it would save his life.

"I'd definitely like that," the dork replied eagerly.

"What's your name handsome?"

"Evan."

"Well, Evan," the woman replied. "I'm Julia. It's nice to meet you," she said as she held out her hand to him.

Evan grabbed her hand and shook it like an idiot. Julia was a pro though. She took her other hand stroked the back of his hands with one long manicured nail. I could see Evan growing aroused. His eyelids looked as though they'd suddenly become heavy. He remained silent savoring the feel of her fingernail gently grazing the back of his hand until she started to speak again.

159

"Evan, as I said, I'm not from around here, but I need a little something to help me take the edge off. Would you happen to know when I could find something like that?"

"We're at a bar. Would you like a drink?"

Julia giggled. "No Sweetie. I want something a little stronger than that if you know what I mean." Julia reached over and squeezed Evan's thigh as she finished her sentence.

I could have sworn I saw the man's libido do a backflip. I struggled not to react. This woman was looking to score drugs! That's why she was giving the dork so much attention and the fool was too dumb to see what was happening. Just as Evan began to respond, I heard a commotion to my right. I turned to see George shoving his grilled cheese sandwich back at Angela.

"Where is the butter? Who the hell eats dry grilled cheese?" he yelled.

"Calm down George." Lauren tried to soothe him.

Angela glanced at me and I mouthed, "Keep calm." I knew Angela had a temper and would not allow George to disrespect her. I also knew she needed her job, so I didn't want her to get too upset.

"Don't worry George," I spoke up. "Angela will send it back to the kitchen and they'll make you another one. I'm sure it'll be right out."

"It better be," George slurred. "I'm hungry dammit."

Angela hurried away. I know George and Lauren thought she was hurrying to get his food, but I knew she was rushing to avoid going off on him.

I turned my attention back to Evan and Julia. Evan was on the phone asking someone if they could bring a white girl to the hotel. Since he was sitting next to a very beautiful white girl, I had to assume that was code for something else, but I wasn't sure what it was. My slang wasn't very strong when it came to street drugs.

When Evan ended his call he said to Julia, "I have someone bringing something right over. He should be here in about ten minutes."

"Will you party with me?"

"Nah, I don't party, but I'll watch you though. And if you want a little after party, I'll be ready.

This time I almost choked on my drink. When did the dork become smooth? I guess that thigh squeeze gave him all the confidence he needed. He was smiling like a Cheshire cat with his eye on the last piece of cheese and Julia was still laying it on thick.

I turned my attention back to George who was now yelling at anyone who would listen.

"You gotta calm him down," I whispered to Lauren.

"You know how he is when he gets like this. Maybe I can take him up to a room to sleep it off."

"Did he get his food? You know he's not leaving until he eats."

"Not yet, but hopefully it'll be out soon. I don't know how much longer I can keep him in his seat, and I need a smoke."

I tried to smile but I'm sure it didn't quite reach my face. Lauren was thinking about smoking when her husband was about to show his whole ass at the restaurant bar. I would never understand people with addictions. No matter how bad things were, they still had to have their fix. It seemed like I was surrounded by addicts. George and his liquor, Lauren and her cigarettes, plus Julia and whatever white girl stood for… what was the world coming to? It was the middle of the week! If they were this bad on a Wednesday, I didn't want to guess what their weekends were like.

Angela returned to the bar with a smug look on her face. I felt my stomach tighten because I knew that look. It was the expression of someone who just got the upper hand. I looked at the plate in her hand. It had a stick of butter sitting on top of what looked to be a cold grilled cheese sandwich. A whole stick of butter! I tried to stop her before George saw her, but it was no use.

Angela slammed the plate on the bar in front of George. "One grilled cheese with butter," she said with an evil smile.

George took one look at the sandwich and his whole face turned red. He grabbed the sandwich and threw it in Angela's face as he yelled, "Would you eat this shit?"

162

I saw Angela's smile fade into a snarl. She was going to jump across the bar. I rushed to stop her as I yelled to Lauren, "Get George out of here!"

It was no small feat, but Lauren sprang into action. She may have been a petite privileged woman but she was no fool. Anyone with eyes could see Angela was about five seconds away from whooping George's ass.

I got around the bar and started to pull Angela into the kitchen. The woman was stronger than she looked but I managed to get her into the kitchen without her touching George. I was going to have to tell the GM about the incident but seeing as how George was drunk and threw the sandwich in her face, I was fairly certain she would keep her job.

I stayed with Angela in the kitchen until she calmed down. As soon as I re-entered the bar area, I saw it was filled with cops. Apparently, Julia was not a prostitute looking to score drugs. She was an undercover cop working a sting. The moment Evan's "friend" showed up, Julia's "friends" stood up. The bar had been full of undercover cops waiting for the drug dealer to arrive. The poor dork who wasn't even a drug dealer or user was now in hand cuffs for facilitating the sale of cocaine. It was the worst Wednesday I'd ever seen in the hotel and I prayed I'd never see another one like it.

Chapter Ten:

Reunited and It Feels So Good

Sebastian came running into my office screaming, "Girl, I got something to show you!" Sebastian gave me the silent treatment for a minute after the casket fiasco but was back to joking and talking to me. He handed me his phone and told me to look at a meme. It was a meme of a famous reality star sitting on top of a turned over coffin. The meme had the picture of this celeb's rival photoshopped over the face of the dead body. The caption said, **this bitch thinks I'm playing**.

"I don't get it," I told him.

He enlarged the image. "Look again. Look at the carpet and background."

I look at it again and after a few seconds I see it. "What the hell?! That's the Asbury Room! Is this Mr. Johnson's casket?"

"Girl, yes! This popped up on my social media feed."

"Them damn kids! Do you think the Johnson family knows about this?"

"I don't know but if not, we sure don't want them to find out."

I check to see If I can find their reservation information. I find the mom's name. "Wasn't the boys names Brad and Chad," I asked Sebastian.

"I don't remember."

I was fairly certain that was their names. I wrote down the boys' names and mom's last name and asked him to look for them on social media to see if they posted anymore photos or videos of Mr. Johnson.

"I gotcha honey."

I hoped Randolph didn't find out. I then realized I never did get the 411 on Mr. Fine Eyes. I pulled the card he gave me out of my desk.

Randolph Realty
New Jersey's Finest
If I Can't Get You What You Need
It Can't Be Gotten

Okay, homeboy buys and sells houses. I went to his business website. I read his bio and saw he'd been a realtor for 25 years. I do the math and determine that he had to be in his mid to late forties. Okay. A little older, but that wasn't a deal breaker. I saw it must be a family business because it said the company had been around for over 50 years. His office was located right in the heart of downtown. I then googled his name and found out he went to Cornell University and that he once ran for City Council.

Interesting. I skimmed through images and discovered that during his campaign his opponent didn't play nice. I clicked on an article that stated that he allegedly tried to falsify legal documents to make it seem his net worth was less than what it was. It suggested that at the time he was going through a messy divorce and didn't want to pay spousal support. I searched further but couldn't find anything that suggested he had kids. I then searched my desk for the program from the funeral. I thought I placed it there somewhere. I then remembered that I had placed it in a magazine that was out front. I hoped someone didn't throw it away. I went to the front and saw a pile of magazines. The hotel gets a subscription of various magazines to put out in what we call our library area. This was a corner of the lobby that had a couple couches centered around a fireplace. I front of the couches was a coffee table where we had reading material like newspapers and magazines. My boss always said he was going to get rid of some of the subscriptions because most people don't read that stuff anymore. They get their info from their smartphone. Besides most of the time the magazines don't make it to the coffee table until we all have read them which is usually a few weeks after they arrive.

I told Sebastian I was going to circulate the mags which means I take the old magazines off the table and replace them with new ones. I gathered the pile on the counter and began rummaging through them looking for the program from the funeral. Where was it? After a few minutes,

Sebastian held up something in his hand and said, "You looking for this?"

I saw the program and snatched it from him. I went back to my office but only after I smacked his arm and told him he needed to go through the mags and put some out in the library.

I looked closer through the program and saw a collage of pictures in it. I scanned them and saw a picture of what looked like a young Randolph with his mom, dad, sister, and another young man which I assumed was his brother. By the look of everyone's attire I would say it had to have been taken in the 80's. I was becoming more intrigued with Mr. Fine Eyes. This was definitely one that mom would approve of.

Suddenly, I jumped when I heard someone barging into the office. It was my boss, Frank.

"Morgan, please reiterate to your folks that they should not be on their cellphones while up at the front desk. I just caught Sebastian playing on his phone."

I think to myself, that was most likely my fault since I asked him to look for our boy graduates and their social media escapades.

"I will speak to the staff immediately," I said. We were probably due for a staff meeting anyway since I hadn't had one in a few months. I liked to have one every other month or so to make sure we were all on the same page and everyone knew what was expected in all departments. I was

one who believed front desk should know what
housekeeping was doing and housekeeping should know
what's expected at the front desk.

On Frank's way out of my office, he told me the auditor
would be there the following day, so he would be in his
office reviewing paperwork. He asked if I had submitted
my monthly reports. I told him yes that they were placed
in his box two days ago. He smiled and walked out. The
one thing I was a stickler about was making sure I met my
deadlines.

I went to check on the front desk and make my rounds. I
passed Sebastian and apologized for getting him in trouble.

He jokingly replied, "That's okay baby you know Frankie
Boy just wanted an excuse to speak to his Danny Boo. You
know he can't get enough of this." Sebastian started
rubbing his body up and down like he was some
Hollywood actress auditioning for the part of Marilyn
Monroe. Even though Frank was married with three kids,
Sebastian swore he was hopping over both sides of the
fence.

Just as Sebastian finished his hilarious Marilyn Monroe
performance, we saw Jacque and Antonio walk by with a
huge banner that said Brunswick High 30th Class Reunion.
Jacque, who knows I graduated from there, jokingly asked
if I am going. I threw a magazine at him and tell him.

"Fool, you know I'm not that old," I scoffed.

He and Antonio only laughed at me as they continued walking down the hall. I forgot we had my alma mater's class reunion that evening. It didn't matter much to me though. All of the attendees would be much older than me. I re-focused my attention on Sebastian.

"Have you found out anything about our wanna be famous boys yet?"

"Not yet, but I have a few more sites to check. I need to check Snap, but you know everything disappears after 24 hours so I may not find much on there. Unless the boys are dumb enough to keep reposting the pics, they're all gone by now. Besides, you know I can't really search while Frankie Boy is here."

I checked out the lobby and made sure everything was in order and that the café had been fully cleaned after breakfast. I looked up and saw Mrs. Stein getting off the elevator looking quite distraught. I rushed to see if she was alright. She was visibly upset so I walked her over to one of the Café tables so she could sit and gather herself.

We sat silently for a minute before she was finally composed enough to tell me what was going on.

"My son has been hassling me about selling the house. Some investment group wants to buy it, but in my heart, I know Harry would not have wanted me to do this. The investors are just going to tear it down. Harry and I worked so hard for that house. I can't just throw all of our hard work away. I know I need to sell it, but I want to see it to a nice family so they can enjoy it and make new memories there. Tommy is getting impatient. He's only giving me a week to find a buyer. I need a realtor fast. Do you know one?"

"As a matter of fact, I do," I replied as I tried to reassure her. "Wait right here while I go get his card. I'll make a copy of it for you."

I could hear her thanking me as I walked away to retrieve the card. When I handed her the copy of the card, she looked at it and said, "Johnson... why does that name sound familiar?"

"It's the son of the woman I saw you talking to last week, the one whose husband died. I believe her name is Carlotta."

She gave me this strange look.

"What's wrong? Would it be a problem for you to work with her son?"

"No, it shouldn't be. Carlotta and I go way back. Remember when I told you about my friend that I would go to Harlem with?"

"Of course! I loved that story."

"Well, Carlotta was that friend. I wasn't completely honest as to why my parents refused to allow me to go back to Harlem. You see, Carlotta and I grew really close, a closeness that wasn't respected back then. We loved each other so much that many didn't understand it. Back then, they would call people like us freaks. My parents got wind of how close we were and forbade me to see her any longer. I was so devastated and didn't know how I would tell Carlotta that we couldn't be friends anymore. Then the riots came, and I had a perfect excuse. I told her we had to end our friendship because of the riots and not because my parents didn't approve. We then went our separate ways and I never saw her again until last week."

Wow! Am I hearing what I think I'm hearing? I would have never guessed Mrs. Stein rolled like that. I could imagine how scandalous their friendship was back then. I was trying so hard not to seem shocked that I had to clinch my teeth to prevent my mouth from hanging wide open.

She continued. "I regret not standing up to my parents. I was afraid that if I had, they would have disowned me and I would have lost everything. At that time, I was in no position to take care of myself financially and was still living with them. I chose money over friendship and as a result my life was never the same."

You could tell she was getting upset so I picked up the paper from the table and handed it to her. "Well let's change that and stand up for yourself now. It's never too late." I handed her my phone and she called Randolph.

It just so happened that Randolph was just finishing a showing in the area and could come by the hotel. He said he would be over in fifteen minutes. I told Mrs. Stein I needed to go check on the front desk for a minute and asked if she needed anything. She said no and that she was going out for a smoke. It wasn't the front desk I needed to check on, it was me. I immediately went into the lobby bathroom and checked to make sure I looked okay. I made sure to put some lip shine on, as my mom called it. I was never really a make-up person, but my mother always taught me that with men it's all about the eyes and the lips.

When I was satisfied with my appearance, I went to the front desk to tell Sebastian about what I just learned. Before I could tell him, a couple approached the front desk to check in. The pair looked like the type of people who kept up with all of the latest trends in fashion but didn't know when enough was enough. They had on designer labels from head to toe that made them look like label whores. It was obvious they'd dressed to impress but had no clue they'd be voted as worst dressed by the fashion police. They were the first to arrive for the reunion. The woman proceeded to tell Sebastian that she was class president and was going to make sure it was going to be a great night. Her husband had a huge box he was carrying that said Class of 1990 on it. He looked like he was thinking about a million other things he would rather be doing. The woman asked Sebastian where the Asbury Room was, and Sebastian instructed her where to go. She pushed her husband and said, "Come on honey let's drop these decorations off and head to our room. I want to get a quick nap in before I meet the rest of the committee to help decorate."

"Have you ever been to a class reunion??" Sebastian asked.

"No. I missed my 10-year reunion, but the turn out was so low we probably won't have a 20-year reunion. That's perfectly okay with me because I doubt I'll go if they do have one."

"Me either. I hated high school. I have no interest in seeing anyone I went to school with unless I can take them into an alley and whoop their ass for torturing me in school."

I was about to give him a quick lecture about letting go of the hate from his past, but he spoke up before I could get a single word out.

"Well, well, well. Look who just walked in."

I looked up to see Mr. Fine Eyes himself looking around the lobby. Mrs. stein stepped in from outside and he went to greet her. I wondered how he knew who she was, but I figured it was a lucky guess on his part. They sat down and talked for about thirty minutes. I began to think of an excuse that would allow me to stay at the front desk so I could spy on them when a bunch of the class reunion guests started coming in. That was the excuse I needed. We checked in about forty guests before we could even stop and take a breather.

I was taking that breathe when Mrs. Stein and Randolph came up to say hello. Randolph held out his hand to shake mine. I quickly and discreetly wiped my hand on my skirt and shook his hand. His hand was so soft. I began to think to myself, if his hands are this soft imagine what his lips would be like. I felt a little excitement in my body, and quickly told my mind to focus on what he was really there for.

"How did things go Mrs. Stein?"

"Very well. Randolph is going to meet me at the property tomorrow morning so he can take a look around. I told him it has been listed for about two months and Tommy has a potential buyer. He is well aware of the urgency of this matter and is willing to do whatever he can to ensure that he finds a buyer who can appreciate and respect my home for what it truly is, a home."

I smiled and said, "Well I am sure Mr. Johnson can get the job done."

Mr. Fine Eyes seemed to enjoy my vote of confidence. He rewarded me with a dazzling smile before confirming the address. I think he was making sure I heard every detail. He didn't need to worry though I was taking mental notes of the entire exchange.

"Mrs. Stein, I don't work until noon tomorrow. I can take you to the house, so you don't have to worry about calling a car service."

"Oh, would you dear?" she excitedly replies. "You know Morgan is such a sweetheart and has been such a blessing to me. She is quite a gem."

"I am sure she is," Mr. Fine Eyes replied with a glimmer in his eye.

Melissa Elizabeth

I felt my face growing five shades redder and looked down at the desk. They said their goodbyes and I watched his fine ass walk out the door. As soon as he was gone Mrs. Stein turned to me and said, "I think he has his eye on you." I gave a little chuckle, but dear Lawd I hoped she was right! That was one fine man I didn't mind looking at me.

Throughout the next few hours, we had more and more reunion guests checking in. I decided to go check on how things were looking with the decorations the class president was referring to. I walked in and saw that the room was decorated with the school colors and each table had a display of pictures, facts, and trinkets representing important invents that happened in 1990. I was secretly grateful she did a better job decorating than she did dressing.

I walked around and saw a table with a picture of Nelson Mandela on it. The caption read, 27 ½ years of imprisonment has now come to an end. Beside it was a table with a bunch of items with prices on it like a toy gas pump with the price $1.34 and the picture of a 25-cent stamp. I then stumbled upon another table that had images of *The Simpsons, Home Alone, Driving Ms. Daisy, Cheers*, and *A Different World*. They even had a table with all kinds of portable CD players each having the name of a number one song from that year including *Vogue* by Madonna, *Ice Ice Baby* by Vanilla Ice and one of my favorites *Vision of Love* by Mariah Carey. I remember many days trying to hit that high note in the shower.

Ok, class president, this is cute, I thought to myself. I noticed the DJ setting up who I recognized from previous events we've had, so I walked over to say hello. I always enjoyed when he came because he knew how to get the people up and dancing and having a good time. Um, maybe this reunion won't be so bad after all.

An hour later, the reunion guests started coming down and the lobby was full of people dressed up trying to recognize people and act like they liked folks they hated in high school. After a few hours, the music was pumping, and folks were drunk and walking around like they were teenagers again. Grown folks knew darn well they were going to have a hangover and body aches the next morning. I decided to go in and check out the scene.

It wasn't my job to check out the reunion, but my curiosity got the best of me. The dance floor was packed with people making fools of themselves trying to either dance or hook up with an old flame. I got a good laugh, so good that I discovered that having not gone to the bathroom in several hours had finally caught up with me.

I rushed to the bathroom and in my haste barged into a stall I thought was unoccupied. It was the handicap one which I make a point not to use, but I really had to go. I pushed open the stall door and got an eye full of the Brunswick High 1990 class president up on the sink having sex with a guy who sure wasn't her husband. She screamed and I rushed out apologizing. Then it dawned on me. Why was I apologizing? I was the hotel Assistant Manager, and they were having sex in one of our public bathrooms.

I cleared my throat and activated my inner authoritarian. "Both of you need to get dressed and leave this bathroom immediately!"

Ms. President came out buttoning her blouse while the dude ran past me adjusting his belt buckle. I looked at her and said, "I see you're making this a great night."

She rushed out the door and I follow behind, completely forgetting about using the restroom. As soon as I exited the door, I saw her husband standing in the hallway. It took less than 10 seconds for him to realize the man that an out of the women's bathroom had been in there with his wife. I watched the calm man turn into a bull who'd seen red.

Ms. Class President immediately rushed to him to try to calm him down, but he was already on the way to attack the man who just had sex with his wife. She rushed out to grab him and as soon as her hand touched his shoulder, he turned around and pushed her away from him. She quickly lost her balance and fell to the ground. I thought seeing his wife on the floor would be enough to stop him, but he just charged ahead.

I reached down to help her off the ground. "I'm sorry he shoved you. No woman should be hit by her husband."

"Don't worry about me. Call the police right now. The man I was with was his best friend since high school. If my husband catches him, he's going to kill him."

Without thinking I released her and let her fall back to the floor. I grabbed my walkie and called for security, then pulled out my cell phone and dialed 911. I knew we'd need all the backup we could get.

The next morning, I was at the hotel bright and early to pick up Mrs. Stein. I was exhausted after the cheating fiasco, but I felt like seeing Mr. Fine Eyes would be all the energy I needed. Mrs. Stein climbed into my call all excited. She clearly misread the energy I was giving off as she excitedly told me about the dream she had about Harry last night. She explained to me that it was a sign from Harry that everything was going to work out with the house. I asked if Harry said anything and she said no. I could see she was starting to doubt whether the dream really was a sign, so I stopped my questioning and turned on the radio. I asked her what music she liked, and she said she always loved the Blues and singers like Billie Holiday. I browsed my music App and found a Billie Holiday playlist. I hit play and we drove silently listening to Lady Day.

As we got closer to her house, I could see Mrs. Stein starting to get agitated.

"Are you going to be okay going to the house after all this time?"

"I haven't been back since the day of the funeral, but I think I will be okay," she said softly.

We pulled up to the house and I saw a silver Range Rover parked out front. "Mrs. Stein I didn't know you had such a great ride," I joked attempting to lighten the mood.

"Honey, that's not mine. What would I do with a car like that?"

I pulled directly in front of the expensive vehicle and watched as the driver's door opened. Out stepped a very well-dressed Randolph. It was a good thing I was sitting because if I'd been standing my knees would have buckled. I didn't know how it was possible for this man to look better each time I saw him.

Randolph opened the door for Mrs. Stein and helped her out of the car. As he made small talk with her, he surprised me by swiftly coming to open my door as well. I was an independent woman who never saw a need for a man to open my car door, but it sure felt good to see a man who proved chivalry wasn't dead.

I thought he would return to Mrs. Stein's side after I got out of the car, but he surprised me by leaning in for a hug. He smelled even better than the last time we hugged and if I didn't know any better, I would have sworn he lingered in the hug a longer than needed. Just as I was pulling back, he whispered in my ear, "It's great to see you again Morgan. You look beautiful today."

I wasn't sure if his voice was always that deep or if he purposely dropped it to try to turn me on. Little did he know, it had been so long since I'd been intimate with anyone that he better be careful before I showed him how happy I was to see him. Not one to look desperate, I simply smiled and told him it was great to see him as well.

The three of us walked up to the house together. For the first time, I actually took in our surroundings. I'd imagined Mrs. Stein living in a mini mansion. Instead, the home was modest. Mrs. Stein unlocked the door and beckoned for us to follow her inside. She fiddled with the alarm as Randolph proceeded to punch some things in on his iPad and take pictures.

Mrs. Stein told me to follow her. We went into the living room and I was taken aback by the beautiful view of the river. The back of the room was filled with glass doors and windows all displaying the gorgeous and peaceful view. I instantly realized why the investors wanted to buy the property. The proximity of the lake and the unobstructed view had to make the property value through the roof.

Mrs. Stein opened the door and walked out to the edge of the property. She just stood there silently staring at the still water. The back porch had two rocking chairs and was filled with flowers and plants.

"This is where Harry and I spent most of our time. We loved to sit out here and talk. It seemed as if the whole world was in a rush, but time stood still when we were out here together."

Even though her back was turned to me, I knew she was crying, so I remained silent. I didn't want my voice to pull her out of her nostalgic moment. We stood there not speaking for about five minutes before she spoke again.

"Harry loved nature. I often found him out here early in the morning watering the plants and putting seed in his birdfeeders."

I looked around and began to notice that every tree in the back had some sort of bird house or bird feeder on it.

"People would wrongly assume the flowers were mine, but they weren't. Harry had a green thumb. He loved his flowers, and the birds were like his friends. He had a name for every one of them.

This place was beautiful. No wonder Mrs. Stein didn't want it sold to investors. I wouldn't have to see any other room in the house because this backyard had me sold. After a few minutes Mrs. Stein walked back to the porch and you could see the evidence of her tears still decorating her face.

"I'll truly miss this place, but there's no way I could live here without my Harry."

I grabbed her hand and squeezed it to let her know I understood what she meant. Though I'd never been married, I could feel the love the two of them must have shared in the home.

Randolph came out and took some pictures of outside. "I think I have everything I need ladies. Can you come by my office to sign the paperwork?"

"Sure. We have time."

"Great. Just follow me," he said as he turned and started back towards the front door.

As we were following Randolph to his office, I told Mrs. Stein that you could tell a lot about a man when you drive behind him.

"How so?"

"Mr. Johnson has stopped at every single stop sign this whole drive, not a rolling stop, but a complete stop even when there are no other cars at the intersections. That shows that he is cautious and values safety. He is driving at a pace the he knows I can keep up with which shows he's thoughtful. I see him constantly checking his rearview mirror to see if I am still behind him which shows he is protective and considerate. He slows down if the light has turned yellow to ensure that we both stop at the red light and I don't have to speed through to make the light before it turns red.   That's a testament to his sincerity and kindness. A couple times I purposely fell behind to see how he'd respond. You saw how he pulled to the side of the road and waited for me to catch up. That shows that no matter what, he will never leave me behind. Plus, he puts his turn signal on well in advance of the turn, so I am not caught off guard."

"Well, I never thought that much about driving, but the way you're talking makes this guy seem like he's quite the catch."

"I don't know Mrs. Stein. All signs are leaning that way."

When we arrived at his office, he signaled for me to park in his reserved spot located in a small lot while he pulled around and parked on the street. Man, where has this guy been hiding? We met him out front and he held the door for us as we entered. His office had a modern design flair but still felt warm and inviting. He greeted the receptionists and introduced us. She welcomed us and asked if we would like anything like a bottle water, coffee, or tea. We both declined. He then asked her to show me to the lounge area while he and Mrs. Stein went to his office. She escorted me to the lounge which had beautiful, comfortable slipper chairs and a television. I had a seat and began surveying the lay of the land.

After about 30 minutes they walked into the lounge. Randolph apologized for keeping me waiting. I told him it was not a problem at all, and I hoped that they were able to get everything completed that they needed. He said yes and would have the property listed that afternoon.

The receptionist came over and told him that his mom was there. He looked surprised but not as surprised as Mrs. Stein. Mrs. Johnson must not have felt like waiting because she came right into the lounge and hugged her son. Randolph then proceeded to introduce us to her and reminded her that I was the assistant manager at the hotel. She smiled and greeted us. I could clearly see that she was uncomfortable and didn't want to let on to Randolph that she and Mrs. Stein knew each other. Randolph then asked if Mrs. Stein and I wanted a tour. I quickly agreed.

"I had a long morning. If you don't mind, I'll just wait here."

"It's no problem at all," Randolph replied. He looked happy to have me all to himself for a few minutes. We exited the room leaving her and Mrs. Johnson in the lounge while he showed me around.

The building was a small storefront that looked like there was an apartment upstairs. The tour didn't take that long because there wasn't much to see. The receptionist area, the public restroom, a staff bathroom in the back, and further down that hallway a breakroom. The last stop was his office which was professionally decorated with a desk and a small conference table. Above the table was a tv which had clips of the pictures he had taken of Mrs. Stein's house.

"Thank you for referring Mrs. Stein to me," he said as he took the seat behind his desk.

He motioned for me to take the seat in front of him. "It was my pleasure. I'm glad you were able to help her. She's starting to feel like family, so I want to make sure she's well taken care of."

"So, you're as kind as you are beautiful."

I blushed. "If I didn't know any better Mr. Johnson, I'd think you're flirting with me."

"You're just figuring that out? I've been flirting with you since the first time I laid eyes on you. I was beginning to doubt I'd have a chance with you."

"And now you think you do?"

"I hope so."

I laughed enjoying his straightforward confidence, but I decided to challenge him. "Tell me why I should give you a chance."

"Well, to tell you the truth, I don't play games. I'm a one-woman man, and you have me so open I was thinking about you when I should have been grieving my father's death. You're the first woman in five years that I've given more than a second glance to."

"I highly doubt that," I countered.

"Would you like to ask my mother or my receptionist?"

"What?" I choked out.

"Seriously, everyone teases me and calls me Monk because they never see me with a woman, but even my mother could tell I was interested in you when we met at the hotel. That's why she's here now. I told her you were bringing Mrs. Stein in and she just popped in to get another look at you."

I knew I wasn't the real reason his mother was there, but I decided to keep that fact to myself. Besides, I was enjoying hearing him profess his feelings for me. I decided to test him once again. "What was so different about me?"

"I honestly don't know Morgan, but if you'd allow me to, I'd love to spend the rest of my life figuring that out."

CPSIA information can be obtained
at www.ICGtesting.com
Printed in the USA
BVHW041406140921
616733BV00013B/386

9 781955 605052